HOW TO REACH FOR THE AMERICAN DREAM

...AND NOT GET IT!

LARRY HYATT

Larry Hyatt
Printed in the United States of America
First printing: October 2013
Muddy Bayou Press
ISBN:978-0985507299

PRINTED IN THE UNITED STATES

Stop!

This is a work of fiction based on events. Use it as a learning tool to know what not to do.

My first day of school, I cried all day. Hell, I cried all year. Decades later I found out why when a friend I hadn't seen since grade school told me I cried so much he remembered what I wore that first day of kindergarten. I was taken aback.

Smiling, he shook his head from side to side, "Larry, you were wearing a white shirt, white pants, red suspenders, and a little red bow tie."

"No wonder I cried. My mother dressed me like a midget milkman."

She knew I had to be noticed. I was going into the world.

"Don't you leave here!" I screamed as I was being pushed through solid double doors, not physically but mentally and with no idea my hysterics would be remembered by someone else for over thirty years. I was emphatic, deliberate, and shrieked, "Don't you leave here!

You, be right here when I get out!" My god, it went on forever.

My mother came down to my level and on the back of her heels with both hands on my shoulders tried to stop a meltdown.

"It's okay, son. You're going to be alright. You can do this. You have to go to school... Look, I'm going to be right here when you get out." My eyes were wide open, waiting to be convinced.

"I'll tell you what. You can sing for me later when you get home. Would you like that?" and she gave a huge smile. Smiling back, I felt better as I tried to catch my breath with airy, staccato inhales.

My teacher took my hand and I was whisked away down a long dark hall. It separated me from my audience. I was scared, but I could feel a tranquil presence in the darkness. Wanting to be brave, I didn't look back. Then I realized I didn't have to. Someone was going to listen to me sing.

Let me explain...

My mother walked with kings and queens, maids and dukes, royalty. (I had an aunt who made every second count, but I'll save the sex in this story for later.)

Mother Mary made costumes for Mardi Gras that pomp and circumstance, "once a year party" in New Orleans that attracts people from all over the world to do what has been going on near the mouth of the Mississippi for hundreds of years, and that's to get drunk.

It's said in New Orleans that the word "Mardi Gras" is French for "throw up in the street," but I thought of it as our livelihood and the chance to meet the blue bloods from the Garden District. They were my connection to the wealthy elite from the many carnival clubs, balls, and dances that would introduce me to the person who will make me a star and get me noticed. And oh, I entertained them.

This little red-haired kid as their court jester would do it all.

Someone would shout, "Hey Larry, do Paul Lynde!" and I would shake my head from side to side and say, "Hello, ya' little cutie."

"Hey Larry, walk like an ostrich!" and with my hands extended behind me I would take long goofy steps across the ballroom floor as the adults would point, laugh, and be amused.

"Now, do the chicken move!" And of course, I did, feeling that this is what should be done. This is what I do. This is what makes them like me. Then, when I had them in the palm of my hand, my mother would say, "He sings, too."

These (and you have to say this through your teeth) "formal affairs" always had big bands with horns and brass, big sounds that resonated through the Municipal Auditorium and into the French Quarter. I pretended they were famous bands from the "forty's era." The band leader didn't always want to let me sing, but he couldn't say no to his boss, the captain of the ball, the guy I had in my back pocket after the ostrich walk.

So in my little black tie and tails I would sing "*Proud Mary*," grabbing hold of the microphone and spinning my arm when it got to the part about "*big wheels keep on* turning." I'd belt it out, "*Proud Mary keep on burning*." I was rollin', rollin' on the river. Everyone would clap, dance, and sing along, and I still remember all those pretty people in black tuxedos and different colored evening gowns, staring back at me, smiling. Mother Mary, she was proud, too.

This got me my television debut.

A well-known New Orleans historian gave me a chance to say the Pledge of Allegiance at a Cub-Scout function. I remember watching myself in our living room on the black and white, my right hand to my forehead with a little boy salute, my mother hugging me, excitedly pointing at the TV.

From there I played the local kiddy circuit. I sang on the show "Popeye and Pals," where I got to eat burgers from Royal Castle. I appeared on "The Retarded Children's Telethon" (imagine the outrage today if they had kept that name) and then the crème de la crème, (big music here) "Johnny's Follies." He was the man.

I was glued to the TV each afternoon after school when this guy appeared. He could sing, dance, carried a cane, wore a skimmer straw hat and had the coolest red and white striped coat. He looked like the Music Man... my kind of guy. My mother was making huge elaborate costumes that cost thousands of dollars, but I wanted a striped coat like Johnny. Better yet, I got to meet him.

Things were buzzing when Mother Mary packed us up and took us to the television studio in the French Quarter. My sister was along, and we were both excited as we held hands and jumped the cracks of the broken Vieux Carre sidewalks. Kellie, in her tiny pink and white ballerina costume, was to dance with her NORD dance troupe. NORD is the acronym for The New Orleans Recreation Department, a city wide entity that taught sports and the arts to kids if they wanted to learn.

For *my* big performance, my mother designed a beautiful maroon corduroy shirt. It looked like a puffy pirate shirt with long sleeves, big cuffs, and it tied in the front, perfect for the sixties. I had on white jeans, and my new white patent leather shoes that I knew would help me shine in the stage lights.

It was time for Johnny to see me sing. Yes, "see" me sing. You see, at this stage of my career, I pantomimed. It's what we called it before "lip-sync." Who would have known back then I had Brittany Spears beat by thirty years. I was an old pro at six, and I was headed for the big time.

The television show consisted of kids, cartoons and hamburgers, two cents worth of meat on a three-cent bun. You told Johnny your name and what school you went to, saw a cartoon, and then saw local entertainment.

While waiting for my chance to sing, standing in the wings, ready to take the stage, I was excited knowing this was my chance to show my hero what I could do. My mother was near, and I was watching Johnny interview Kellie's group in the bleachers on the stage, when this tall, slim man, holding a white poster, said in a high pitched voice, "You're on, Go! Go! Go! Larry. You're on! Knock 'em dead, young fella."

I smiled at my mother, took a deep breath, and moved to my place at the center of the stage. I looked out into the studio, and it seemed enormous. The three television cameras were right in front, towering above me, pointed downward, one-eyed robots, eyes open wide. My heart was racing.

When the lights dimmed, I glanced at my mother. She winked at me, and I heard the introduction to my number, "Put on a Happy Face" from the musical *Bye, Bye Birdie*. I was counting down the beats, and just as I started to sing, off to the left by my sister, I heard a loud noise, a commotion that made people's heads turn. Two girls in the NORD dance troupe started screaming, and it got everyone's attention. One of the little girls in a fit smeared mustard from the hamburger on the other's costume, and she was ready to have a complete conniption. In turn, the little girl grabbed a handful of blonde locks, and it started a kiddy catfight right there in the studio.

Dancing school pink erupted out of the bleachers. Everywhere you looked pint-sized ballerinas dived for cover. Little girls were yelling and crying, jumping all around grabbing for their parents, while mothers and fathers were running into the chaos to save their kids. Johnny threw the microphone down, tried to help, got his hat knocked off, and they trampled it. He then ran for cover, tripped over the wires, fell on his face, and took refuge in the control room.

"Put on a Happy Face" was still blaring in the background, and I could see all the mayhem in front of me. You see, I didn't leave the stage. I kept singing my heart out, "slapping on a happy grin" and "spreading the sunshine all over the place." I was on the "Johnny's Follies

Show," and I was not going to be denied. I was putting on my "happy face" because I knew this was important, to do well, to make people like me, and get them to notice. That's what felt good.

When things died down, I was allowed to sing again. The studio was now quiet, all but two of the adults gone, licking the wounds of their young wounded cubs. The tall skinny man stayed. He applauded loudly and very enthusiastically when it was over. Mother Mary graciously thanked him.

I remember that day and the excitement of my chance to shine. It gave me a complete and utter contentment that I couldn't yet describe. Looking back, it was as if something or someone was propping me up, to be in front, to feel the energy of a room and people in it. I became fearless.

My mother put me to bed that night, and as she pulled the covers to my chin said, "I love you so very much." She said the word "so" like it came from deep within, an unconditional love that made me feel safe and protected, the feeling I associated with appearing on stage under those lights.

My mother was right. They noticed me. Little did I know my life would be "so" much more?

Red Foxx, Princess Diana, and How I Learned To Love Garbage

I was raised by women; my mother, grandmother, aunt, and sister. It taught me to never underestimate the power of estrogen. It helped me understand that women left to their own devices can successfully love, nurture, and instill extreme fear.

My mother didn't intend to raise us without my father. It was just something that happens, "divorce." It left Mother Mary, a single parent in the sixties, to dig deep into her soul and show me, Kellie, who is fifteen months older, and my brother Jimmy, who is five years older than her, the ways of the wondrous world.

Now I understand why my parents couldn't make their marriage work. They came from two different worlds. My mother was opera and my dad was bowling. I had a lovely childhood with the best of both worlds. I was lucky enough to grow up on both sides of the street.

My dad was a cross between Dean Martin and Red Foxx, an attractive ladies' man who liked to get a little crude, a night owl who enjoyed laughing and cutting up with his friends. You know the joke, Jack Daniel's, Glen Levitt, and Tom Collins. At night while driving in our family car, my father would turn the headlights from low beam to high beam, and then, say "Hello, Jim Beam."

My father would have been the most comfortable in life being the fifth member of the Rat Pack. He wasn't a drunk. He worked very hard for what he had. I think he just loved to cut up, laugh and party, and we hindered that. He was a bartender, who for years paid his dues working weekends in popular nightspots, and ended up owning his own restaurant and bar on "West End," a beautiful and very popular place built over the water on the west end of Lake Ponchatrain. He bought into it and remolded it for the '84 New Orleans World's Fair with money he got from a lawsuit from when he was employed by the New Orleans Public Belt Railroad, and a boxcar door he was working on fell on him. It crushed him and almost killed him. The World's Fair ended up a financial disaster, but he did love owning a nightclub. That was his identity, what he wanted to be.

He left my mother when I was six, went back when I was ten, and left again two years later. He was confused over the love for his identity and the love for his three children. He was a weekend dad when he made it at all. I remember playing next to a suitcase for hours in front of my house, Mother Mary trying to get me inside.

"I know he's on his way, mom. He just had to work late. He's on his way. I know it. I'm just gonna play till he gets here." When it got dark, my neighbor from across the street came over and sat down next to me. He spoke for a short while about how sometimes "Dads" get tied up with things they have to do, and a person being older brings on things that have to be done, things a person can't get out of. He finally said, "Larry, I don't think your dad's coming. Your mom needs you inside."

I didn't take those incidents lightly. I found out later my mother sent our neighbor and then eventually sent me to therapy where I learned the basics; "It takes two to fight," "You don't have to have the last word in an argument," and the one I came up with while in "children's" group therapy, "Screw this. You kids are crazy! I'm just not going to be unhappy anymore!" I resorted to self help. "Good God, It's a miracle! He's cured!"

As a teenager my father and I spent many great times together even after he married Lauren, who was years younger than my brother. I learned two things from my father not living with us. You can live without people you love, and don't get married because you love someone, get married because you can't live without them.

He was a sturdy man. While walking into his house early one morning after work, he was shot in the chest by two men who he thinks planned to rob him. With a hole clean through his back, he ran up the stairs with his young wife and called the cops, ran down the stairs to see where the shooters went, and ran back up the stairs to check on his wife. When the ambulance got there, he said, "You're going to have to carry me. I'm not walking back down those stairs." That episode also nearly killed him.

Then, two years later, he went home from his restaurant and found Lauren dead in the hallway of his East New Orleans' home. A gun was lying next to her. When my father, I, and my siblings, came back from making funeral arrangements he got out of the car next to the mailbox, grabbed the mail, and walked inside. Standing next to the kitchen table, while going through the mail, I noticed he had an expression I've never seen before. His face that showed sadness, now showed confusion.

"It's a letter from Lauren," he said.

He ripped the end of the envelope and blew into it. That's how my dad opened his mail. He took out the letter and started to read. Enthralled, he slowly carried it to the adjoining living room and fell back, easily on the sofa, three sets of eyes riveted his way.

"What is it dad?" my brother asked.

Looking down at the letter and in a breathy tone my father said slowly, "It's a suicide note."

He turned his wrist and studied the envelope. "She mailed it two days ago."

Slowly, he lifted his head, looked straight at the wall in front of him, and as if trying to comprehend, said again. "Two days ago," his words coming out as if to ask a question but still a statement or observation.

From across the room, he turned his head toward his three children and said, while shrugging, as if he didn't understand, "She blamed me. She blamed me for her problems. I couldn't make them right. I thought I could fix them."

I felt sad for him, since I also had blamed him for many of my problems, and started to dig deeper into why even parents can rationalize bad behavior to their children. I wouldn't know for many years.

That episode didn't kill him either, but it sure changed my father. He didn't take his kids for granted after that, and we ended up with an unspoken, mutual agreement. He didn't call me, and I didn't call him, but when we saw each other at family functions, birthdays, and weddings, everything was forgiven. That was the relationship I had with my father. I forgave.

As a young man my father was not only tall, dark, and handsome, he was fit, and an athlete. He was a semi-pro football player who worked for NORD running the neighborhood playground, the playground around the corner from our house, so he could be closer to his kids. I had the extreme misfortune of being a coach's son who was too small to be a great athlete. So, in his wisdom he taught me strategy, how to play smart, never say, "Can't" and "never, ever, give up." He drilled that into me. Luckily, my brother was the athlete and took some of the heat off the family member with the twinkle toes. My father wasn't thrilled with my passion, but he knew people noticed.

He died at age seventy-six in the same house Lauren did. He was still a part-time bartender. That's how much he enjoyed his identity. I'll be damned if that's the gene I got.

On the other hand, Mother Mary was a cross between Joan Rivers and Princess Diana. She could "walk the walk" and "talk the talk" with the best of New Orleans' elite. She was a pretty, fiery redhead who would dazzle them with her creative ability, charm, wit, warmth, and savior-faire. Then, only when it was appropriate, she could quietly tell you a great dirty joke. She was lady about it. It wasn't "There once was a man from Nantucket." It was just blue enough to make them say, "Oh, Mary," and love her even more. God she was good. She made me admire all single women who raise their kids on their own. Actually, she made me love all women with the same passion I had for the stage.

My mother was raised middle class with an older brother, who was well-educated and admired greatly by his peers. A younger sister who was educated as well, professional women of the sixties, both in a world where the glass ceiling was prevalent. Mary, a middle child, wanted her identity to be a dressmaker.

Mary got her start by designing and making wedding dresses, scarves and accessories, anything to make ends meet, and at twenty-seven made a Miss America mantle to be worn at the crowning on national television. She parleyed that into a contract with a carnival club.

Being a costumer played right into my intended life in the theatre. By ten she could give me a piece of ribbon, crape paper, and a kazoo, and I was doing the first act of West Side Story.

From there, Mother Mary added more carnival organizations, and it became the family business. She designed and executed for twenty-seven krewes throughout the city, Gulf Coast, and South Louisiana. My mother, sister, and I would travel to the Gulf Coast on weekends to fit the costumes on the members for Mardi Gras Balls in that area, me singing the whole way. The song Edelweiss from the musical "Sound of Music" was my mother's favorite. She taught it to me at 8 years old. I wish I had a nickel for every time I sang that song from the back seat of my mother's station wagon. I made it my own.

Our house was a factory. I would come home from school and find ladies at sewing machines all through the place. During carnival season, members of the courts would come to the house for their fittings, and I learned not to park in someone's driveway because the wealthy elite thought they owned mine. I had to park so far down the damn street; it took a plane, two boats, and a cab to get to my front door. The neighbors weren't thrilled either. We were all thrilled when my father added a second story during his two-year stint, and eventually, my mother moved the business to a large warehouse and called it "Designs Unlimited."

As time went on, I think my father just couldn't hang with my mother, probably intimidated by her new role as a polished New Orleans businesswoman, and that was the final nail in the coffin. My father was a bad boy she loved more than anything in the world, thus the second chance, but she had three kids, and we would become her life.

She was my stage mother, my biggest fan but understood the process and didn't ever get in a director's way or build me up to them. She would take me to auditions, plays, and shows and would nurture what she and I knew both knew, I liked this, being noticed.

Before Mary started her costume company she, worked at a fabric store in Metairie, a suburb of New Orleans. I also worked there weekends and summers from the time I was ten through high school. It took an hour and a half and three public transit buses to get there, but I didn't mind going to work. The majority of the time I couldn't work from looking at all the pretty women. All types of women sewed back then. They were young, old, big and little, some drop dead gorgeous and some, downright peculiar.

When I got older, I found out some of those peculiar looking women were actually men buying costumes for the drag shows in the French Quarter. Plenty of the gay carnival clubs bought their fabric there to make their costumes for Mardi Gras, and strippers came in all the time to buy fabric for burlesque.

I liked talking to Miss Roxy; she was real, buxom, had a high pitched, squeaky voice, and always called me her "little dawlin" as she pinched my cheek. She would tell me, "One day, I'm gonna steal ya' from ya' momma, and put you in my Cupie Doll collection." I had to ask my mother what a Cupie Doll was.

Roxy made me feel liked. She sometimes brought me little gifts, always had chocolate, and thought the world of Mother Mary. Everyone there did. And let me tell you, this working environment was an interesting place to grow up.

First, there was the owner who was a round-bellied fellow who loved his beer and had one when the day was over. Actually one hour before. He reminded me of the sidekick cowboy actor from the old westerns who talked kind of high. Not Gabby Hayes, the other one. He knew his business. If he said something was in the warehouse, it was there. The man actually taught me how to find things. Just keep looking, and looking. And then look again. You'll find it. He admired my mother's strength as a single mother and would have helped me in any way he could. He did by letting me work there.

There was his wife, who was five feet tall, 350 pounds, and didn't take any shit from anybody. She was tough. When people complained about the service, she'd walk away from them while they were bitching, go to the telephone and start dialing the number for the Better Business Bureau. She would then hand the receiver to the customer and say, "Here, tell it to them." I always imagined that the BBB would come over and throw the customer out. They also had a worker they called "Princess." Need I say more?

Princess had been working there since day one. She was a very nice old lady, but she was always trying to get out of work. It would have been easier for her just to do what she was paid for. If a customer would ask her to cut some fabric, she would say, "Wait, let me get my scissors," and slowly shuffle her tired feet as she walked across the entire length of the store to get her scissors. When she got them, she would return duplicating the walk, while customers impatiently tapped their watch. All the other employees kept their scissors in their work apron.

There were two little old gray haired ladies, each about four feet tall that were also employees for many years. They were twins, Jean and Joan. I couldn't tell them apart. No one could. When I would see them together, I would think of the lyrics from the Santana song, "With Jean and Joan and who knows who?" because nobody knew- who. Customers constantly got them confused, which was hilarious. Years before, they had an argument with Princess over which time employees should go to lunch. It was huge. The twins didn't speak a word to Princess for decades. Imagine working for twenty years without speaking to a fellow employee.

They had Camille, a gay guy, who was the funniest man alive. He had quips and puns and blasted everybody. He constantly had me laughing. I looked forward to seeing Camille every day. He said to me, "The best part of being perfect is that you can talk about everybody," one of the first lessons of comedy. Of course he didn't mean it, but it sure was hard to "cut" funny, especially when the person you're making fun of can't hear you. Sad thing about him though, he was one of the first of my mother's friends to die of AIDS.

There was Mother Mary, and finally, my first crush, the owner's daughter, the reason to go to work. She was older, and I liked that, about twenty-five, and curvy up top. Me, being eleven, I would get embarrassed when Camille would catch me ogling her and would say to me, in his flamboyant voice, "I see you looking at her. You like 'em large, huh? Those, bodacious ta-tas? I know what you want. You want to rub 'em. You want to lay your head on em." He knew I liked her, a lot.

The owner's daughter was street smart, hip, and downright fine. She was confidant and way out of my league, but I couldn't tell that to my adolescent hormones.

Her eyes were big and bright, and she looked like a blonde haired Ann Margaret. Her husband had died, and she was a widow so there was no man around to scare away my fantasy.

I would follow this woman around the store like a puppy, straightening the racks of fabric that were close to where she would be, only to catch a glimpse. I hoped for big shipments to arrive so the warehouse would fill up with empty boxes. A full warehouse meant that we would have to go to the city dump. That meant I could be alone with her in the van. "Me and my baby at the dump," I thought that was so cool. There I could make my move or at least bring up how I felt in conversation. My brother had some penthouse magazines under his bed, and I would sneak a peek at the forum letters. That's what was going to happen to me. If it could happen to a group of men dressed like the "Lollypop Guild," it could happen to a short, red-haired kid who could make people laugh.

One particular Saturday morning I got the courage to go for it. We jumped into the loaded van; she lit a cigarette and was making small talk.

"So, when is your next performance?"

"Oh, well, everyday is a performance."

Her head stayed straight, but her eyes looked at me. She gave a crooked smile.

"So, how's your mother?"

"She's busy with Mardi Gras; I don't get to talk to her much."

"Consider yourself lucky." The cigarette dangled from her mouth giving her a slight muffled sound. "I see mine all day. I can't keep anything a secret. She knows everything about me."

"Yea, that must be tough," I said.

"Yea, but I guess we're lucky to have good mothers. I just wish mine would let me live my own life and stick to hers. Their generation just doesn't get it."

"Yea, I know, they just don't get it. They ought' a just get out of our life."

"Stay out of your life? Are you sure?"

"Yea, stay out of my life, Damn it."

She laughed. I saw just her eyes again. I was making headway.

We pulled into the dump on Airline Hwy, and as she backed the van to a ramp that had a drop off of about fifteen feet, I noticed the place was loud from all the machines packing the trash and garbage. Big trucks where all around, and I could hear their air-brakes squeak and gears grinding. You could smell the odor from all the debris.

We proceeded to unload the boxes, and she was speaking, but I couldn't hear her words because of all the noise. As her lips moved, I did realize just how beautiful she was. I remember thinking her hair was "pretty." The day was sunny, and it shined.

She had on a loose fitting, cream-colored, silk blouse that buttoned up front with a short collar. The ensemble was dead on. (Hey, give me a break. I knew crap like that. I worked in a freaking' fabric shop.) The top buttons were undone, and it made her even sexier. That day her usual pair of tight faded jeans seemed more snug, and her smile seemed more radiant. As we threw the boxes into the pit, everything seemed to be in sync.

There was one big box left to toss. We looked at each other, and each grabbed an end and both flung it as hard as we could. That's when the clouds opened, and the "God of Sanford and Son", "The Lord of the Trash," smiled upon me. Her right breast fell out of her shirt for the entire world to see. I couldn't believe my luck. I even saw my first nipple.

God, it was a perfect breast. It looked round, and soft, and hung there, for moment, and wiggled just a bit, like Jell-O. It was the most beautiful thing I had ever seen. The look on my face must have been complete disbelief. On her face, complete shock.

In one smooth motion her left hand crossed her chest, cupped her breast, and placed it delicately back in her bra. It was so fluid it looked like a dance move. That's when I turned away in embarrassment and lost my footing. I slipped on the discarded boxes and fell on my ass right into the 15-foot pit. She started yelling for help. I started yelling for help. The men who worked at the landfill came running. They stopped the machine that packs the garbage, and they had to fish me out by putting a ladder into the pit.

When I reached the top, I was completely covered with funk. My pride was gone, and I never felt so stupid, especially in front of the girl of my dreams.
I smelled so bad that on the way back to the store I had to ride in the back of the van.

On the way she would glance back at me in the rear view mirror and ask, "You alright right back there?" I could see the framing of those eyes in the rectangular refection that showed just a hint of a blush, possibly feeling she knew she gave this kid the thrill of his young life. I just smiled gleefully, looked out the window, and muttered, "Yea, I'm fine."

That day didn't turn out exactly how I had it planned, but I'll tell you this, that glimpse of her right nipple comes to mind every time I take out the garbage.

Older and A Lot Less Cute

By age twelve and in seventh grade, I already had eight years of performing experience. I played the monkey on a stick, the willow in the woods, the village idiot, and the lead in school plays, sang at PTA meetings, Christmas pageants, numerous city-wide talent shows singing "Proud Mary," and created my own shows for the neighborhood in my back yard.

I won awards for being the best altar boy but not because I had the calling. I looked at it as another way to be on stage. I'd ring the bells. I'd carry the cross. When the priest wasn't there, I would get on the altar and pretend I was in the movie, "The Ten Commandments," and could part the Red Sea. I put on the black and white cassock and surplice, which my mother handmade, of course, and extend my arms out pretending I was Charlton Heston and summon the Lord.

"Behold the power of God. I am the way, the truth and the light, and get your paws off me you dirty stinking ape." Okay, I did mesh up all the dialogue which made the other altar boys think I was a Looney Tune. But, I relished pretending to be someone else.

Now at this age, adolescence, something started to happen. I was getting older and a lot less cute. Gone were the days of doing the ostrich walk and the little Irish jig. I had to start developing my talent. I did have "something." People kept telling me so, and I enjoyed that feeling immensely. This was also the time I graduated from elementary school in New Orleans East and got bused to a desegregated school across the tracks.

In Orleans Parish, in the early 70's, students had music class five days a week. The focus on the arts was enormous back then, and Thomas Jefferson Middle School had some teachers that were extremely talented. I would now say before their time. Mother Mary hired one to give me voice lessons after school. Jerry Edwards, my first of many music teachers, showed me a film called "Introductory to Opera." It taught "story and music together." It hit home, big time.

The opera was Pagliachi, the story of a clown who is heartbroken because he found his wife with another man. He, as heartbroken as he is, must go on stage and entertain the crowd despite his sorrow, anguish, and shame. Grand opera stuff and I related to it. My parent's marriage was breaking up, again, and I too found it hard to put on my happy face. But even more so, opera was acting and singing together. That meant I could sing and I pretend was someone else all at the same time. Jesus, life couldn't get no better than this.

Mr. Edwards started teaching me the basics about voice, musical scales, breathing from my diaphragm, standing up straight and dropping your jaw. Mr. Edwards molded this group of twelve and thirteen year olds into some talented "school stars," doing variety shows that had big production numbers, great costumes, and music ensembles. They got the school band involved. Mother Mary even made red, white, and blue vests for the finale where we sang patriotic songs to a packed auditorium. It was like living in a perpetual episode of the television show Glee or the movie High School Musical.

I learned a great deal from these teachers, a great basic understanding of how and especially why; the show must go on, to bring joy and laughter to others.

This was when entertaining became something I wanted to do more than anything else. Something I had to do. Be it for the notoriety, the pats on the back from family members, or the sheer adrenaline rush of being on stage and in front of an audience, my focus now was to "make it." I tried to get in every show I could and along with that came a price and some very embarrassing moments that would trigger a sequence of events that would rear its ugly head and teach beyond the classroom.

Performing in a Christmas show consisting of the band, the choir, and the dance team, the choir was to sing classic Christmas songs and different students would take turns singing solos in between the choir's performance. It was a standard Christmas show for the school in an auditorium of about 700 people.

On this particular evening, the auditorium, decorated in red and green, was lit like a Christmas tree. The holidays were near, school would be dismissed soon, and everyone was excited from having Christmas parties all day.

During the show, the choir had just sung the last notes of the song, "O' Come All Ye' Faithful," a boisterous rendition with all of us singing with abandon. I was to then walk to the microphone and sing, "O Little Town of Bethlehem."

I walked to the microphone and noticed the soloist before me was about a foot taller and the microphone was too high for me to sing. Once again being short stung, but by now, I was a seasoned professional. When the audience started to giggle, I remember telling myself not to get rattled. I tried to fix the microphone, but I couldn't turn the lock in the middle of the pole. I heard more giggling. I remember telling myself not to get rattled. I tried to fix the microphone, but I couldn't turn the lock in the middle of the pole. I heard more giggling. As I struggled to unlock it, a teacher entered from the stage's right wings. She couldn't fix it, and I heard laughter. When Mr. Edwards walked on and gripped it tightly, it finally moved, all the while the audience amused by my lack of strength. I knew I was short. Now I felt a bit weak and a bit embarrassed. I looked down from the stage at Mrs. Leblanc, my music teacher and accompanist, and she looked up and smiled as if to ask, "Are you ready?" I nodded, smiled, and was ready to go

Now, let me catch you up on things. The song that I had just sung with the choir was "O Come All Ye' Faithful" and the song I was about to sing, "O Little Town of Bethlehem," start on the same vowel, "O."

I heard the teacher play the soft, slow moving, melodic introduction of the song "O Little Town of Bethlehem," but I, in my infinite stage wisdom, sang the song, "O Come All Ye Faithful," very boisterous, the way "O, Come All Ye Faithful," is to be sung.

Upon reaching the end of the first phrase, I realized I made a huge mistake and stopped, but now the audience, dumbfounded, had the impression that "this idiot really made a mistake." I looked down at Mrs. Leblanc. She was looking up at me with a very strange expression, and her head was moving back and forth, very fast, seeming to ask while moving, "What the hell was that? What on earth did you just do?"

Completely embarrassed, I could feel the sudden shock of heat and humiliation on my face. The blood rushed to my head and made it spin. The entire auditorium was laughing, and my feet suddenly started to make short up and down movements from right to left. I kept telling myself, "Get a grip. Get a grip. Get a grip," but, I couldn't. My breath was short and staggered, and I backed away from the microphone, dipped my head, and shut my eyes, the darkness giving me a reprise. I felt sweat on my face.

I lifted my head when the auditorium started to quiet down and being a stage trouper, I was ready to begin again. Again, I looked down at Mrs. Leblanc and nodded to start over but it was too late. My knees started shaking, my voice started quivering; my whole body was out of control. I was in complete fright, but damn it, I was not going to give up.

"O Little Town of Bethlehem, with its soft, slow, consuming melody came out in a high pitched shaking mess that went on the entire song. It's the first time I felt my knees shake with fright. I was so scared the vision in my eyes shook from side to side, like a camera shaking back and forth, and it went on and on and on and on. I was devastated.

When the song was over, I was still shaking as I walked back to my place in the choir. I can't even remember what happened on stage next. I do remember after the show teachers were saying it wasn't a big deal. I also knew I had walked up to the microphone and sang the wrong damn song in front of the peers I would have to see when I returned from the holidays.

That incident would become a defining moment in my life. Not for the sheer devastation of a childhood screw up but for the consequence. After that incident, of complete embarrassment, I became aware that the stage could take away the most beautiful of feelings in the world. The stage, being noticed, being propped up in front was now not my utopia. It was now a contradiction of what I love, what makes me whole, and my biggest fear, the fear of failure. On one hand, the stage was beckoning, "You must do this, to be who you are," and another voice inside saying, "Don't, or you'll become the idiot, the buffoon, the laughed at."

The fear of being in the public's eye is what I intended on thrusting myself into, and like a fool, I wanted to become a masochist.

When you get in front of people and perform as often as I did, I guess the law of averages catches up to you. I knew mistakes would be made, but with me, the performing side always won. I wrote it off as, "At least they know who I am," which seemed to get my ass kicked.

In the early seventies racial tensions were a bit high to say the least. Schools in New Orleans were on the evening news with tension between the races. Riots were breaking out, and my brother would come home and tell us of pick combs in the hair and fists in the air, Black Power, and it scared me. Our family didn't really care. We were gluing rhinestones to dresses. Black people sewed with us each day in the rooms we added on the house to expand my mother's business. We were "live and let live people," artists. In fact Mother Mary would let black and white gay men into our home and show them how to make their costumes for the gay carnival balls. This was at a time when their own families scorned them. Their mothers, fathers, siblings, even the community wouldn't let them be a part because of their sexual preference. I was taught not to care about race or religion or if you were gay. We just wanted to earn a living doing what we do best. But, the violence did trickle down to us.

Once in grammar school I was helping a teacher pick up books he had dropped breaking up a fight. As I was bending down, a black kid kicked me in the face. I'll show you the chipped tooth. That was the first time I ever blacked out. No pun intended.

Another was when I was delivering advertisements door to door, in a black neighborhood. That day I had a wide brim straw hat that my grandparents brought back from a cruise in the Caribbean. I wore it a lot back then. I really liked that hat.

As I was going from house to house, some black kids approached me and the person I presumed was the leader of the group said to me, "That would be a good grass cuttin' hat," right before they swiped it off my head and beat the living shit out of me. I learned then that you can get the living shit beat out of you, and it won't kill you.

Believe me, all that crap is water under the bridge, kids stuff. But I will tell you this. Back then black kids didn't like short, funny, red haired dudes. Actually they liked them even less on the third Monday in January, Martin Luther "The King's" birthday. Let's just say his message of inclusion didn't include me. In my realm young black kids were still pissed, really pissed. I hoped I eased their pain.

After a rehearsal one day for a show the school was doing for Mardi Gras, I was walking to get on the school bus. I was well aware what day it was; they had events all that afternoon. I was alone and a bit uneasy.

Walking down the left side of the hall along the lockers to exit the building, I'd say about twenty black students had started my way. (It was actually six.) I was committed to going forward. I didn't want to be a wimp, so I kept on, knowing they couldn't kill me. They surrounded me.

"Hey! Santa, you fucked up."

"Where are your reindeers, Santa Claus?"

"Look, man, just let me go."

"White boy, you sing like a little girl."

"Hey white boy, you a sissy."

I tried to go around them by moving to my right and toward the middle of the hall. I couldn't, so I stepped back. I couldn't back up either. When I tried to go left, I was slammed into the lockers. That's when I felt the first punch.

As I was being pummeled over and over all I could think was to hold my head down and travel along the lockers. While covering my head and moving down the row of lockers, I noticed the perfectly straight line of combination locks, hanging, all with the black center and silver loop, all the same, all down the line, and now blood being splattered on them. I could feel something warm around my belt. I didn't know what it was; all I wanted to do was get out of the beating. It struck me as I was being struck that the warm feeling was pee in my pants. That's when I saw a silver knob on a door and opened it to get away.

Of all the places I pick to seek refuge, it's in a classroom full of girls having a student government meeting. When I burst through and look up, it looked as though every girl in the damn school was in there all looking at me with a bloody nose and pissed jeans. Some started screaming and jumping around. Some ran out. Others were trying to help me. I remember a teacher yelling, "Go get the principal." I was so embarrassed that I had wet my pants in front of the girls that I wanted to go back in the hallway and take another beating. I wanted to be anywhere but be in that room with all the "smart chicks."

They sat me down and quickly locked the door for what would be only a few minutes but it seemed like hours. I was embarrassed sitting there waiting for the principal to arrive, using my hands trying nonchalantly to hide my crotch.

Things quieted down. People were now talking amongst themselves, and as I sat turned to the window, an older black girl who had left early from rehearsal came over and handed me a tissue. As I wiped the dried blood from my nose, she looked down at my pants, shook her head, and said, "That's nothing, Larry; my drunk ass brother does that all the time." It didn't stop the embarrassment, but it did make me chuckle.

"Thanks for the napkin."

"You know I met your momma. My uncle makes those pretty costumes with her."

"No kidding, really?"

"My daddy don't like'em and calls him names, but my momma loves her brother no matter how he is. I like him, too."

We smiled at one another, and she went back to the group.

Today, I know it was all part of growing up and besides, I think getting my ass kicked actually taught me how "not" to treat people. It was beat into me.

Brother Can You Spare a Dime

Are you the type of person who won't ask for anything? You have the mentality that if you accept something you owe something in return and don't want to be indebted? You feel their acts of kindness, which should make you feel good, would fall short because people have gone to trouble and that makes you feel like a nuisance.

So, possibly you've developed an, "I'll make it on my own" type of existence. "I'll do without," is what you tell the world. "If I can't afford it, I don't need it," you say, as if it's a penance, and doing without will prove to everyone, "I'm on my own."

For me it began when I was thirteen years old. My parents had divorced after separating twice, and I was happy just to see my father, a weekend dad, who I missed quite often. He had a very good job, worked nights, and the courts had him paying child support for my older sister and me. My brother had reached eighteen and passed the threshold for giving money for the depositing of one's sperm.

Every two weeks that child support check was due. It was one hundred and eighty dollars for two slightly teenaged children living with their single mother. The exact cost is seared in my brain because often my sister, or I, had to ask for the check. We would take turns to balance the uncomfortable humiliation that we knew was inevitable. We knew he could afford it; it was just that at that point we both learned that it was a pain in the ass to ask for money.

We would never do this the first thing when he picked us up on Saturday. We knew we could spend a great day together doing the things that kids love to do such as going to a skating rink, seeing the latest movies, or eating at fast food restaurants, and didn't want to spoil the day. My sister and I enjoyed the cool things we got to do with my father and because my mother couldn't afford it and had to work on Saturdays, we never wanted to make waves. A divorced father's luxury is dealing with children who are now scared of losing not only their father but his love, too. Or, what if we ticked him off and made him angry like the old days?

My mother hated asking us to ask for the check, but we were mature enough to know she needed it. I'm sure she felt he should remember. The fact that it cost him less in the long run should have reminded him. He had mayonnaise, ketchup, and bachelor crap in a refrigerator, inside a trailer with minimal furniture that wasn't in the best part of town. He couldn't have been paying more than if we were living with him but that is only in hindsight. Sometimes we'd even lie and tell my mother we forgot to ask for the check, Knowing, our dilemma, many times she went along with the lie. My mother never badmouthed my father, not to us, and this went on for two more years.

At fifteen and able to drive, the every weekend pattern of my father going to his former home had subsided. We would visit his. I still relished his company. He was my father, a man I looked up to for what he instilled in me. It was a Saturday. I was in his new home with his new young wife, and my day with him had come to an end. It was time to ask for "The Check." We were sitting at the kitchen table.

"Well, Dad, I guess I got to get oughta here."

"Okay, Well, it was good to see you, son."

As I heard the sound of the wooden chair slide back under the table, I remember thinking, "Please, Dad, remember the check. Remember the check. Remember the check." I turned to the front of the house. We were approaching the door. My father said, "Okay, son, well, it was great to see you. You're always welcome here."

I turned to him. We hugged, and I said, "I love you, Dad."

"I love you too, son," was the reply, and I felt the three pats on my back and a stronger embrace that confirmed his feeling.

When I reached for the door knob, I had the sinking feeling that I would not hear the much-anticipated words, "Oh! Here, give this to your mother," so I turned to him and said apologetically, "Mom asked me to ask you for the check."

My dad stopped a beat, gave a 'tis" sound, shook his head, and walked to his desk which was in the room next to the foyer. He abruptly pulled his checkbook from the right top draw and started writing. That's when I heard the words that changed my life.

In a mild disgust he wrote the amount, $180.00. Then, as he wrote out on the check the obligatory words, "one hundred and eighty dollars" he said without lifting his head, "Sometimes I think this is the only reason you come here."

My heart fell into my stomach. I blinked real hard.

When I opened my eyes, he was signing the last part of his name, and it felt like a gut punch as I heard the perforated edges of the paper pull away from the stub. He handed me the check. Not wanting to take the hit, I said, "I'm sorry, Dad. Mom asked for it."

"Aw, don't worry about, son. You kids are good kids."

He walked me back to the door, we hugged again, and I left. All was forgiven, but when I got back to the car and drove away in tears, I swore I would never ask anyone for anything, again.

In one's life, this is a trait that can come back to haunt you; it haunted me because later in life he received millions in a lawsuit, money people all around grabbed and groveled for, but I didn't take. I was told many times, "Ask your daddy for it." I said no. I have a dream, and I'll make it on my own.

One day, you might meet the person or people who can send you on a path that could put you right in the middle of what you love. In my case, it was searching for the dream I'd had as a boy.

I now know that there is nothing wrong with having rich parents who can send you to Los Angeles, New York, or even Branson to start a career. Nine out of ten times that's how people from small towns make it. My trait was a fuck-up.

Today, I don't mind accepting gifts from people. I enjoy getting gifts. It lets me know they like me, and as some might say, I need to be liked. Plus, I like having more stuff.

Actually, acts of kindness toward me thrill me, and when I accept a gift, I don't think that person has an ulterior motive. Although, one should be careful of the people who reward them, then constantly let them know about it.

I once heard my father who has given me many gifts since then complain about my mother's father, who he said, "would give you the shirt off his back." My grandfather would have. But the end of my dad's complaint was "but he's going to let you know about it every time."

Now, I don't remember my grandfather ever throwing any acts of kindness into anyone's face. Maybe that was my father's self-consciousness of leaving his wife and three kids, but I certainly understand the concept and there's the freaking rub.

I can accept anything you want to give me, whole-heartedly, ever so accepting, graciously wanting, and extremely thankful, but don't throw it in my face. Don't you realize that I wouldn't ask if I didn't need it? That I haven't dug deep down and asked because I think first, you might have what I'm asking for, and second, you might give it to me, and now third, you won't need it back anytime soon?

Of course, you have to know who you want to loan things to and whom you don't and the first rule of lending to a friend is "don't." But please consider this, most people don't want to ask and some might not want you to give it to them.

NOCCA Knocks, Rocks, and Shocks

.   Upon getting out of Thomas Jefferson Middle School alive, I had my high school years planned. I would join the Abramson Senior High School Choir like my older brother. It was an award winning choir with four-part harmony and not just a two-voice chorus like the one I left. Then, in my sophomore year, I would audition for the New Orleans Center for Creative Arts, a new performing arts high school that at the time was only open to sophomores, juniors, and seniors. I heard about this new school through Mr. Edwards. I was actually included in the promotional pictures they took when they came to Jefferson to take the shots of students in various forms of the arts. It was my first modeling job, and I loved it, another step on my way to being noticed.

The life plan was working. I'll take a hiatus from voice lessons for the first year and get ready for NOCCA. (NOCCA is pronounced with the long "O".)

The morning of my first day of high school I hurriedly took the stairs to the third floor auditorium, jumping the steps two at a time and on seeing the piano got that familiar, comfortable feeling. When I saw the choir director sitting at his desk, "it was on."

I recognized Mr. Wax from seeing him at shows I attended in support of my brother. Mother Mary made us go to all of each other's functions whether we liked it or not. I still hear her voice, "Damn it! We support one another. We're a family for Christ's sake." I always wanted to tell her, "Then, let Christ be there."

Walking across the classroom to shake the teacher's hand, knowing I was getting in, I said, happily, "Excuse me, sir; I'd like to audition for the choir."

"Just let me sing Edelweiss and show me where to stand, old fella," was what I was thinking.

The tall, very skinny, white haired director, whose head was enormous and reminded me of volleyball on the end of a stalk of sugar cane, said eloquently in a deep baritone voice, "I'm sorry, young man, that won't be permissible. My experience tells me you're not ready."

"Um, what… do you mean? You haven't… heard me sing."

"Well, I became acutely aware while you were speaking. Your voice hasn't changed."

"Oh, well, I didn't know that was…anything…. to think about."

"Oh! It's well an issue. Where would I put you?" Then he gave a low guttural giggle.

"Umm, how about in the choir, you maroon?"

That again was what I wanted to say. Instead, I was dumbfounded. This was very new to me. I was puzzled, shocked really. I never expected this. I'm a trained vocalist.

"No, I'm sorry," he said. "Until your voice changes, you'll not be singing with us, young man. I would have to put you in with the girls." Then again he gave the giggle, a low, deep, guttural, four sounded giggle, heh, heh, heh, heh. I'll never forget that giggle.

The choir director didn't allow me in. I sang like a bird but higher than everyone. A beautifully trained falsetto voice that he felt was not only a problem but a deal breaker.

Dejected, walking out the door, it hit me. No wonder when I answered the telephone the person on the other line asked, "Is this Kellie?" Until then, I had no idea my voice could be mistaken for a girl.

Without even given a chance to sing, I realized I was going to have to figure this out. I was confused, but I knew I had my whole career ahead of me. "To hell with them. I got NOCCA. I'll make it later," was my thinking.

"What the hell am I going to do?" I could join the drama club and be at the bottom of the food chain for parts, but that would only be when they had plays. Plus, I wasn't singing. That's how I was going to get to the top. That's what I had done since I was four. I was a singer, a good one; at least that's what they told me.

Today, if this had happened, a parent would have the school board's ass. Years ago you didn't bitch about the school system being unfair. Life isn't fair, and you just sucked it up. I was born in the back end of the baby boomers; whining wouldn't come till my generation had kids. Some friends suggested I go into Student Government and that it was basically a popularity contest. I, wanting to be noticed, went along.

I ran for freshman president with the slogan "Get High with Hyatt." That synched the "weed-head" vote. Instead of paper signs, I tapped into Mardi Gras and made big elaborate banners. The mascot was a commodore and used royal blue fabric with silver sequin trim. The shining silver against the royal blue velvet could be seen down the long halls and outside; in the sun it reflected to across the street. My sister was designing Mardi Gras costumes by now, so she designed the banners. Mother Mary had the supplies, and I had a carnival campaign.

Interesting enough, the two girls I ran against were close friends, so their group split their vote. Students noticed me from being on stage at Thomas Jefferson, and the ones I didn't meet remembered me as the guy who got his ass kicked and pissed in his pants. I guess anything to be noticed. That year I became Freshman President.

It was a lot of fun being freshman president, but I sucked. I wanted to have fun, and I wasn't a leader, possibly a hint I didn't take of things to come. Plus, I was enjoying the status quo, and the whole time knowing it would be a one-year stint before I got to NOCCA and the real fun begins.

In the summer after my freshman year, I auditioned for and easily entered NOCCA's vocal music department, "high" balls and all.

The New Orleans Center for Creative Arts, at that time, was an experimental public school. They had one like it in New York and made a movie about it called "Fame." But the difference was that at NOCCA, you didn't remain at the arts school all day. At NOCCA, students went a half a day at their "home school," so I was lucky in that I still had ties to the neighborhood, my bros, my peeps, my close friends with whom I shared my childhood.

One of the most enlightening and mind building aspects of NOCCA was that it was a magnet school. It attracted students from all over the school districts of New Orleans which made the diversity huge. Some of these creative young people were rather freaky, plenty of long hared, weird creative types. Some only wore shoes to class. They were young yet interested in politics and world issues, the future politicos of the day. They intrigued me, made me want to learn about world issues, expanded my mind, and I learned once again not to judge people by how they look.

The building itself was a remodeled elementary school from the thirties, painted bright colors of red, yellow, and blue. The colors wrapped around walls and columns. We called it the basement. It was the ground floor.

The splashes of color exploded into the stairwells and through the halls and on the doors of the classrooms. The building was located in the Garden District, just blocks from Audubon Park, and allowed us to take breaks to enjoy a spacious area in Uptown New Orleans, and feel the city's history and see the stately architecture. Or we would go to "Riverview," another park, just blocks away on the bank of the Mississippi River that allowed us to see the churning water, relax in the grass and talk of our destinies or perhaps pretend we were something more than just kids trying to carve out a life for ourselves. We were special, young artists, performers, and creatives. We were living proof not all youth is wasted on the young.

On the school grounds we had an outside amp theater where students could perfect their craft on bright sunny days. In cool weather, the sun shining through the oaks and onto the performers were inspiring, smelling the trees and magnolias, or other flowers' fragrances added to a school day that didn't feel like one. At first, I thought it pretentious to see students, especially the males from the theatre department, roam the halls in black leotards and tights. They looked like mimes, to me, silly. A look I didn't understand. Then I saw the pink leotards of the nimble girls in ballet and thought a guy could get used to this shit. The jazz and classical students played their instruments wherever they felt the need. I met people with perfect pitch, much smarter, but all gracious and helpful. Magnificent sculptures were in the schoolyard, and the student's artwork was constantly changing on the wall. Other students would analyze and interpret the work. To me it looked like a weird looking rose but to them, "it was humanity trying to bloom and become the civilization it should be."

"Damn! I didn't get that. Let me look a little closer to that shit. Oh yea, that's what it is."

It was a world of the arts, the world that had already consumed me.

Each student was in a discipline. You took theater, vocal music, instrumental music, classical music, jazz, dance, creative writing or visual arts. My sister was also enrolled and was taking Visual Arts. Kellie was now working for my mother, who years before when I started voice lessons began taking art lessons.

We both were now moving along nicely. Kellie was an up and coming young artist who did fantastic work around New Orleans, and we were both now in the same grade. We became very close having to travel the city together. She wasn't just an older sister anymore. She was a good friend, and she was making me a better young man.

I liked my new friends at NOCCA. I was singing opera by day and belting out Led Zeppelin in my friend's garage by night. My musical taste was also getting eclectic, and I liked combining the styles.

When I first heard the song "Bohemian Rhapsody" by Queen with the opera sound in it, I thought I was going to be known not only as the guy who pissed in his pants but the guy who shit in his pants. It was opera and rock together, Wow! The school was making me think more intellectually, too. I had culture, Shhh-eee- itttt!

My plan was to use NOCCA to get me to the top. I had some on the best music teachers in the country. I was going to school with some of the most talented prodigies in the city. My voice teachers were known national musicians; NOCCA had the top professors in their field at a high school level all teaching us how to become stars. If you're chasing the dream, you couldn't miss with this place. It was the shit.

Local theaters were excited about NOCCA, too. Theater directors knew where to go to get young talent. My first major production outside of school was at the Le Petit Theater in the New Orleans French Quarter. What theatre history that was! They wanted me and a black student from NOCCA, a fellow sophomore to perform in the musical "Shenandoah," a civil war musical that was popular at the time. They needed a young rancher's son and a young slave. They called NOCCA, and a classmate and I got the part. The father of my black classmate wouldn't let him play a slave. Another young man named Wynton Marsalis was called, and we played opposite one another.

The cast and crew were about 60 people. It was full of producers, directors, choreographers, lighting directors, and set designers. They had massive sets that would rotate and become completely different. I was in awe, and I got to perform with Wynton before he became the great success he is today.

These talented people touched my life. This young kid was now getting a good dose of life in the theatre, and the many different personalities that make up the arts.

Men in the ensemble were talking about their "husbands." I remember one guy bent over in front of the group to put his pants on and showed his ass. Another one said, as weird as can be, "Look Mom! The Grand Canyon." I still think of that when someone bends over in front of me.

The actresses were quick changing in the wings and showing their bodies. When one of them realized, after about five shows, that I wasn't supposed to be in the wings at that time, she realized what I was doing and started to screw with my head. When her top was off, she would turn to me and shimmy. Her breasts would shake, everyone would laugh, and she did it for me. It was harmless from across the room but it was "titties," and "I liked titties."

Cast members talked, laughed, and cut up, and no subject was off limits. Everything was fair game, not like today. When the curtain fell we would go to restaurants and bars in the French Quarter where we would all laugh some more.

I felt very comfortable with entertainers. These friends understood what it took to really have a passion for the arts and love the lights. I belonged with them, the theatre community who in ways truly becomes a family.

I was studying the arts by day and hanging out with theater people at night. My life was beautiful. It's what I wanted to do forever and I was getting volumes of knowledge.

In that show I got advice from the director that I still live by, a New Orleans theatre icon. To have acting lessons with this guy is worth its weight in gold. Many before me have had the privilege to absorb the words, directions, and strategic movement of the stage from this man and there I was getting a master's class.

Wynton and I had a scene together, and the director was working with us after everyone had gone. No one was in the building. We were on the stage; the theatre seats were dark. The only lights were those from above. The hardwood floor was lit. The theatre had a slight echo. Wynton and I were seated together, and the director, facing us, was feet away in another chair, leaning forward, his deep voice consuming. Enthusiastically using his hands he said, "What the scene lacks is energy. It's got to have fire. It's got to have energy."

My eyes were wide; he had every bit of my attention.

"You kids have to feel it, deep inside, and let it come out. I want you to feel that energy," and pointed toward the empty seats, into the darkness, and said slowly and convincingly, "So they can feel it, too."

My God was I moved. My soul stirred. The hair stood up on my arms.

I learned at that moment that every time you're appearing on stage you have to have "energy." A light went on in my head and at I that moment I understood. Even when you're on stage completely still, you still need to generate energy, for the darkness, that tranquil presence, and the audience that came to be entertained.

No more did I want to perform for just myself. It was for others.

Friends, use the energy. All your passion, all the love of the stage, all the adrenaline, let it shake you from the tip of your toes through your body and into your head. Energy! Energy! Energy! I will now live by it.

That got me an audition for the movie "Pretty Baby" filmed in New Orleans. It starred a very young Brooke Shields. They needed a young red head to play the part of her friend, "Red Top." I was older, but I still looked young, and my voice hadn't changed. That could be my break.

The audition was in a hotel on St. Charles Avenue at Lee Circle. I got through the first audition because I had more "energy" than any kid in the place, and there were plenty of kids. I knew the secret word, "energy." Hell, I was a lightning bolt. They called me back to read for Polly Platt, the writer. (Cue the energy.) They then called me back to read for the director, the one and only French director, Louie Malle. I finished reading, and he said in his French accent, "Very good." Then he said to the writer, "Maybe, we can make him a little older."

I was elated when she said, "Possibly?" and shook her head up and down in approval.

I'm freaked. They talked some more then said thank you very much, and I left the room. I walked out in the hall, and Mother Mary was sitting in the hallway smiling. I knew she could hear me through the door. She shrugged and said, "All we can do is wait. You did sound good. Where did you get all that... electricity?"

I never heard another word, but I learned so much from that experience. I knew I was on my way to something else, something bigger. The next shot would come. If I can grab the attention of these people, I was going to have energy in everything I do. Energy was now my drug. But in my junior year at NOCCA, it all came to an unbelievably, screeching halt.

Larry's Law

In my second year at NOCCA, while in my weekly private vocal class, the voice teacher told me I should get out of music and become a businessman and basically, I didn't have what it took to succeed. I was confused. I've been singing since I was a child. Did I suck? I wasn't good enough? Did he not see I wanted it more than anything? It took me an hour and a half to get to the damn school each morning. I caught a freaking transit bus that stopped at every corner. Okay! It was filled with girls in different colored plaid skirts but still, an hour and a half. Maybe he thinks my voice is too high? Students made jokes about it.

"Hey Larry, if you were born in medieval times they would have cut off your nuts to keep your voice high." Yuk. Yuk. Yuk.

"Maybe this singing thing isn't for you; it takes dedication," the teacher said. "Maybe you should be a business man." Then it happened.

The vocal music class consisted of me, a white girl, and about ten black students. We all got along. That wasn't an issue, and it seemed the teacher was training us with what he felt was the best way to train high school students. But, it was with more religious and spiritual songs than opera. I learned lyrics such as "Every time I feel the spirit moving in my heart I will pray" and "Elisa rock shout, shout, Eliza rock coming up lord." I sang it like Mr. Whitebread.

I really wasn't relating to the Gospel music, but I went along because this is what I do. I sing. We did however learn Italian art songs and that was very close to opera.

Finals for the semester were coming up, and we had to memorize the Italian translations. Naturally, how can you sing with feeling if you don't know what you're saying?

I do have to let you know my teacher was blind. He couldn't see a thing. It didn't hinder his teaching ability. I liked the guy. He had talent that would blow you away, and impressive. He could smell gum the students were chewing from a hundred yards away. And hear? Jesus Christ! He'd tell us to go outside then come back and tell him what "key" it's raining in.

On test day, for the finals, no one was prepared. All of us discussed this before the test so all the students decided to have the translations right in front of us on the desk, the whole time we took the test. The teacher couldn't see the papers on our desk because he was blind so everyone would easily pass the class.

Enter "Larry's Law." This law seems to be the one law I've come to live by my entire life. I learned a long time ago that no one died and left me king. That is why....

IF SOMETHING CAN BE SCREWED UP, LARRY HYATT WILL SCREW IT UP.

The law has actually kept me from making more stupid decisions in my life than I already have.

I cheated on that test with everyone else in the class, but I didn't write the translations verbatim. I paraphrased, so not to get caught. The other students did write them verbatim. I flunked the test, didn't maintain the "B" average, and got thrown out of NOCCA.

I was devastated and felt like a complete moron. I couldn't even cheat correctly. How piss poor is that? I didn't tell anyone of the deception, and believe me the students were thankful. They had to maintain grade point averages, and if a college found out they cheated on finals, their scholarships would have come to a crashing end. Just like a tragic opera I wanted to be a part of. Go figure.

I look back today and think maybe I should have said something. Maybe I should have come clean. Maybe we would have all gotten expelled, but I doubt it. I just don't know. I don't know why I didn't say something. Maybe, deep down I wanted out.

When I told my mother I didn't maintain a "B" average and wasn't going back the following week, she was extremely disappointed, and I really felt like I let her down. I loved that school, and it was the best thing that I had going. I actually felt like I let my whole family down. They were proud of me, and I liked it when they would tell their friends about the next show Larry was doing. It's what parents do when they're proud of their kids. They brag about them. Even my dad was proud.

I went back to Abramson High School full time and started working on my next big performance, getting my ass back into the ultimate performing arts school. I got my chance about six weeks later when that teacher happened to resign. I guess he didn't see it coming.

You see, once again, the women in my life came through. Kellie was still at NOCCA so we had an inside track as to what the school was up to. She came home one day and told us the vocal teacher had left, and the vocal music department was getting another director. I seized the moment and spoke to the new teacher about why I wasn't in the school. I mentioned that the former teacher told me I wouldn't make it as a singer and to be a businessman and that made her uncomfortable.

"At your age no one knows what a student's potential truly is."

This new teacher also noticed all the students "trumpeted" their lips when they sang. Since the former teacher was blind, he wasn't concerned with how we looked on stage, and how the heck would he have noticed anyway. He was concerned about how students sounded. The new teacher was well aware of the fact that a person has to look at least pleasurable, if not extremely good-looking, while performing and that your looks would start to play an even bigger role in the future. She told us of this new medium she had heard about in New York that was making its way to television called the "music video." Who knew it would become a huge obstacle for the ugly singers in the world?

Before I returned, she did ask the other students if they had a problem with me coming back. They all agreed, whole-heartedly to give me another chance. If I had been them, I would have, too. I had plenty of time to think about what had happen. I was back in. I wasn't far behind because I only missed, six weeks.

The new teacher revamped the music school, and in a very interesting observation, I was told, possibly, my voice wasn't allowed to change. The extensive training didn't allowing the voice to mature. I really don't know how true that could have been, but hey, maybe she was on to something. I still sang higher than the girls. I could easily sing as high as Michael Jackson. I'm now 16 and can hit some very high notes, but in the opera world, it ain't gonna fly. Like an idiot, I wasn't training to be a pop star, and no one was coming near my cahoonas'.

Then, while on Christmas break, singing at an assisted living home for white hair and glasses, my voice cracked, the most beautiful of sounds to my ears. The torment would end, but be careful what you wish for. I immediately started singing in my lower register, my beautiful falsetto, that caught everyone's attention was gone.

I started training my new lower voice for the deeper sound it had now become but low and behold, I didn't have the range. I started struggling to get the notes that before I had achieved with ease. I couldn't scream Led Zeppelin. I didn't have the range of Caruso (Pavarotti wasn't famous yet), and I was caught in the middle with only a pretty voice. This was traumatic. I seriously thought about changing disciplines, go into theater and learn to act but decided to trudge on. With don't quit ingrained in my head I would try to develop the voice I was left with and still make it to Julliard. I'm a good singer. At least that's what they told me.

A great learning experience, I must relate, was at the end of my junior year when all the returning students had a chance to audition for the touring group "Up with People." If accepted, I'd get to travel from town to town with a bunch of very perky singers and dancers spreading good cheer to the many towns that needed uplifting, positive, family entertainment. "Up With People" is a cross between a musical revue and the Brady Bunch. I wasn't an exceptional dancer, but I moved well and could easily bang out the steps "Zoom" was going to give me. I thought what the hell. I could parley this into something good by putting this on a resume, getting noticed outside the city, and possibly to a bigger touring company.

The audition was after their performance at the Municipal Auditorium. Right outside the French Quarter, the place where I performed numerous times as a kid for the carnival balls.

The audition would be one song and a short reading from a script. I rehearsed with my teacher for a month the song "Edelweiss" from the musical "Sound of Music." I've sang it a million times; it really showed off my voice because it was a lovely song in my range, and everybody knew I had a great shot at touring with this group.

It just so happened, that afternoon, I sang at NOCCA for the entire music school. The teachers, my peers, and school officials were packed in the auditorium; it was a special show for the vocalists who sang solos of Handel's, "The Messiah."

"The Messiah" starts with very elaborate music, crescendos, and has magnificent operatic type stuff. It's not an easy piece. When performing, you need plenty of breath control during long vocal passages with extended arrays of notes, but that day my adrenalin was pumping knowing I would sing for some of the best music students in the city. My solo was a heavy, dramatic song, but I nailed it, really and truly nailed it. Never have I sung so well.

After the performance, when my classmates and teachers got to critique me, one of the professors said in his sophisticated professor voice, "It was very "belcanto."

I didn't know what the hell that meant, but I knew it was good because during the performance when the music called for me to sing pretty, I sang angelic. When the song summoned the Lord, I used a glorious tone. When I sang about sin, I made it dark and mysterious. I walked out of that performance ten feet tall. Even my peers were impressed. I was amazed at how much they liked it. That night I was going to sing "Edelweiss" and pull off an American Idol audition like no other. I was going to be a freakin' "Brady."

During the "Up with People" musical show, it was surprising and very comical to see this group was more "Brady" than the Bradys.

My God! It was so white bread the black students from NOCCA didn't think white people could act like that. It looked as if the Sesame Street puppets had spawned and created Barney kids. It was sickening. They swayed from side to side, with their heads going side to side, and their shoulders and arms going back and forth. It was quite scary to know that if chosen, this was going to be a summer spent in the throngs of good, clean, wholesome fun. Either that or these teens drank and smoked weed in every freakin' hotel rooftop and stairwell from PBS to Disney World. No teenager is that perky. Either way, I was going to pull this off.

After the performance it was time for the audition. Approximately thirty students, males and females from all over the area, were ushered into the audition room and lined up along the wall all eagerly waiting to join the group. When it was my turn to sing, they called my name, and as I was climbing the stairs to the stage, I had this fantastic idea. "To hell with "Edelweiss," I was going to relive my wonderful performance of four hours earlier. I was going to sing "The Messiah." It was pure genius. As Simon would have said, in his English accent, "You've got to make each song your own."

I took my place, and when I was ready, I nodded to the judges sitting at the table. When they nodded back, I took a deep breath and belted out the first words to "The

Messiah." I got through two lines and the director put his hand in the air and said, "Stop! Stop! That's enough. Thank you… next." Simon couldn't have done it better. The difference was this guy's accent was very "gay" and looked eerily like Charles Nelson Reilly as he rolled his eyes and flipped his hand when it got to the top of his gesture.

My eyes shot across to my other classmates, and they had that "WTF" high school look on their faces. The look that says, "What the hell did you just do, you moron?"

They just kept staring at me, slowly shaking their head back and forth in disbelief. That's how I remember them, wide eyed and shaking their head. I didn't know what to think. No one had ever stopped me in an audition. I'd seen it done to less talented people, and it wasn't good.

I went back to my place in line dejected and embarrassed. I was finished. "Up With People" said, "Up yours with people." Larry's Law strikes again.

When I got back to school Monday, we told our teacher of the audition, and she wanted to kill me in a very loving way.

"Why the heck did you do that?" she asked. "Larry, you were a shoe in. You have that type of voice. It's for musicals. Why on earth did you do that?"

"I did so well Friday I thought if I could do it again, I'd be in."

"It was a totally inappropriate song for that audition, completely inappropriate. Oh! Larry! Larry! Larry! Oh my, goodness… Larry!"

I learned a valuable lesson that day. You have to be aware of what you're auditioning for.

When I watch the show "American Idol," I relive that moment with every singer who gets in front of the judges and is told, "That's the wrong song for you." Or, hearing Randy say, "Oh dawg, that was a terrible song choice for you, man," and is sent packing with his tail and his ego between his legs. I didn't get in "Up with People," but neither did any of the eight students from NOCCA, the premier performing arts school in the city. Maybe they thought we would be on the rooftops and in the stairwells.

A performer exists through auditions. Sometimes that's the only time you need talent. The audition is what gets you the part. Get the judge, casting director, or even a flunky at the door to get you to the next step. Ask any non-working actor in the world.

To this day auditions are a bitch. I love them because it gives me a chance to perform. I hate them because it could mean the rejection I fear. I go to them because it lets me know I'm still in the game. Sometimes I don't know if I'm pitching or catching but I'm still in the game.

The Senior Finale

In my senior year at NOCCA, I would gain even more knowledge when the entire music discipline combined to create a choir. The instrumentalists didn't relish the singing, but it did create a high school group unsurpassed in the state. I then started playing piano.

For the "Class of 78", It was also time to start practicing for our senior recitals. Each student to receive a diploma had to do a solo concert for a final grade; each student's very own show that would consist of Italian, German, French, and English art songs. I was ready. As usual, I had it all planned.

I would wear a black tie and tails, stand in front of a grand piano in a big auditorium and light up the room. My family and friends would attend, and my glorious voice would travel acoustically perfect through the third and fourth balconies. I would take the stage to thunderous applause; my reputation preceding itself, sing three Italian songs then leave to bigger applause. Return to the stage and sing three German songs and leave to greater applause. I would reenter, sing three French songs and leave to stupendous applause. And finally, to the stage once more and sing three of the most poetic arias in English. There wouldn't be a dry eye in the place from singing the aria from "Pagilchi" where the clown must go on stage after catching his wife in the arms of another man, the song that so thrilled me as a boy and sparked the desire to entwine my voice and acting together. At the end of the performance my family, friends, and the invited dignitaries, from all over the world, would rise up in a standing ovation. Thunderous applause again would be heard in the heavens. My recital was going to be an "A +." I was going to finish my school career on a "high note," and go on to study at the "Met." I was chasing hard, and it was a few short months away. I could feel it, taste it. I was beating the odds.

By January of that year, the colleges started calling. I sent applications to the music schools of Julliard, Eastman in New York, talked of going to Michigan, Florida, Loyola/ New Orleans, The University of New Orleans, and Tennessee. Tennessee State actually came to NOCCA to hear us talented, young folk sing.

I wrote the book on auditioning musically. I would never forget "screwed up with people," so I sang beautifully for each college. I was on my way. But there was another audition that was going to influence the direction of my life. An audition that all students who want to advance to higher education must participate, the SAT. The Student Aptitude Test is the audition that will let colleges all around this entire country know that academically I haven't grasped a damn thing in the last four years. In fact, I was to find that there was only one thing had come between me and a four-year scholarship at Julliard, just one thing, high school.

I don't remember what my SAT score was, but I think I got a couple points for filling in the bubble sheets in a pattern like a "Lite Bright." I spelled out the word "piss off" because I knew I was going to fail.

I was a "C" student, didn't know shit, and that is not what gets you noticed. I had too much singing and dancing and not enough reading, writing and arithmetic. Was that what that music teacher meant? He could see me much better than I thought he could. Actually, he saw right through me.

If I get to speak to young people who enjoy the arts, I tell them this story. It's the same thing you tell kids who excel in sports. The top of the pyramid is very small. Study the academics. I could eat for days at the "bottom" of the food chain. I wasn't there anymore.

One by one, I got the letters. One by one the grades didn't jive. I noticed I didn't receive a letter from Loyola in New Orleans. I called them, and by a wild coincidence the music teacher I spoke to had a name uncannily close to mine. He remembered my name and the audition but said the grades aren't there. I begged him to give me a chance. He said, "I can give you a shot. You're too talented to not have a shot." I worked it out with the student loan department and got a state grant to pay a whopping $1,500 a semester. Mother Mary came to the rescue with her unconditional love. You have to love the women in our family. I would start Loyola in the fall. The last thing to do was sing my recital.

That day was like no other. I dedicated my senior recital to my grandparents who were so wonderful to us growing up. They and my aunt were the reason we had the rest of the things we needed through our young lives, the extras like cookies, the name brands, yearbooks, and class rings. My family taught me blood is thicker than water.

The recital was in a conference room in the Public Library on Read Road across from the high school. Not the big grandiose auditorium with the balconies that I had planned. I sang and everyone applauded each time I took the stage, and also when I was finished each language, just like I had imagined they would. It wasn't thunderous applause, but it did fill the room and me with a feeling of accomplishment. It was my show. Overall, "I done good."

The French part got a bit freaky. I forgot the French translation so I started making up sounds like Maurice Chevalier. No one noticed except a friend of my mother's who spoke the language. He got a huge kick out of hearing me sing gibberish. The damn translations came back to haunt me.

I did get to stand next to a grand piano and that was awesome. I even wore a tuxedo. I chose not to wear the black tails. It was the gray one I rented to go to the senior prom. We could save money that way.

We had wine and or'dourves so it became a (say it through your teeth) "catered affair"; Mary's idea.

It was really a great day. I sang well, and I got my "A+." My family and friends signed a white guest book.

After cleaning the conference room and with most people gone, we had to give the venue back. The kisses, hugs, and all the "Larry, you were wonderful" were over. I walked over and gave my mother a big hug, and of course a kiss to thank her, the kiss representing all the guitar lessons, singing lessons, piano lessons, and even sewing lessons. I thanked my sister for giving me a girl's point of view of just about everything, teaching me how to treat them, how not to treat them, where to take them, how I should dress when I'm with them, and how to act around them.

I thanked my brother for all the fishing and hunting trips he readily took me on when dad was too busy, the love of rock and roll, and the times we spent alone in our room at night trying to figure out how he got this far without him killing his little brother.

We all hugged, and it seemed to linger longer then our group hug usually last. My mother said she'd finish and that I should go with my friends. She was proud of me. I could tell, "Proud Mary."

I was glad I had her, the woman who most influenced my life and the woman without whom I wouldn't be.

My high school music career was over. It was time for closure, closure to a wonderful "young" world of singing and dancing, acting and performing, laughing and crying, and of course, learning, all the while receiving the basic knowledge of the arts, where and how to stand, sing through the back of the room, and have energy, especially, when standing still. It gave me a solid foundation and the understanding of what I wanted to do with the rest of my life. I wanted to be a star. The sky was the limit. I wanted my dream.

By the skin of my teeth, I made it to a bigger pond. But again, I'm at the bottom of a food chain.

Upper Education

The Loyola University School of Music was much like NOCCA, but now the sound of music was everywhere. Music came from all directions, piano chords from behind closed doors, beautiful voices in unison emerging out of buildings, the mesmerizing sounds of string quartets resonated as musicians practiced in the grass. Sound you could see swirling under the majestic oaks of Audubon Park.

All through the day the people of music carried their tools, musical instruments and music compositions, written meticulously or haphazardly on musical staffs, moving from one space to another, violins and cellos, trumpets and saxophones, microphones and electric guitars. People whose whole life was music hurriedly tried to perfect the tones and pitches that stirred their souls. They would be teachers, conductors, and rock-stars. I wanted to be in the opera, to sing while acting on a stage, under bright lights immersed in the drama of love lost, infidelity, death, murder, and war. And, there was no doubt in my mind, I was going to make it.

At NOCCA, people came from all over the city. Loyola had students from all around the world. I had a friend from England who played classical guitar, a friend from South Africa who played the violin, and a friend from Canada who played the drums. His father was an Ambassador for Christ's sake. This was better than high school. I was walking among adults with the same dream, and it was time for me to make a choice, a tricky one, for I knew Larry's Law could rear its ugly head.

The music school had three programs, and each student had to select what type of degree they wanted. There was "Music Education," where you would receive a degree to teach, but by this time, I had plenty of music teachers who had me doing the damnedest things. One would say, "Think of the voice coming from the back of your head." Another, telling me, "Think of the sound coming from right behind your front teeth." Another who said, "You should feel as if it's coming out of your chest." One teacher had me on the floor with books on my stomach to strengthen my diaphragm; another made me breath like a gorilla to learn how to expand my lungs. One very large female teacher told me to sit completely naked in a cold tub of water and sing all the scales facing the corner of the wall to hear the acoustics. Right, like I'm going to do that? By the way, it didn't work, and damn that water was cold. Teaching didn't thrill me.

'Music Therapy" was working with children and adults less equipped than most to rule the world. Through music, your job was to make these people's lives more bearable and in doing, make the world a better place. I wasn't ready to give up stardom, a dream, and plenty of money for a better world. I was going places.

And finally, "Music Performance," where you'll have a degree that states you went to four years of college, and you can sing. It doesn't say whether you sing beautifully or not, but it is a degree. So I figured I'd take the path of least resistance. Yeah, that's me. The teacher was right.

Actually, I just wanted to get better at singing by increasing my range. I didn't need a plan "B." I was going to be a star. I did achieve a few notes higher in my range my last year of high school, but I still had that light airy tenor quality with a baritone range. That's not bad. But "Pavarotti," I was not.

I selected Music Performance and found out the hard way, that a person with a Music Education or Music Therapy degree can always perform and make money while having that career, but when you get a Performance degree they won't let you teach or make the world a better place, ever. Another lesson learned too late. Ah, Larry's Law.

I took twenty-one hours of credit my freshman year consisting of voice lessons, music history, music theory, piano, Italian diction, and opera workshop where I sang in productions of "The Barber of Seville," "Don Pasqualle," and "Don Juan." I got to study under the wonderful Arthur Cozenza who was running the New Orleans Opera. More master classes with an icon, while "acting and singing at the same time." I was in heaven and had one of the best teachers in the city. I excelled. Again, I can't fail.

All that music was a dream, come true, but I also had English 101. There was no math, no science, and no world history, just plenty of music and English Composition. It would be a piece of king cake. I wrote my first English paper the first day and got the news, "Johnny can't read," and "Larry, you can't write worth a crap." I was heaved into remedial English the next day. They actually came and pulled me out of class by the ear. It was my first year in college, and I wasn't smarter than a fifth grader.

Oddly, I did well in that class of under achievers and that's when I met one on the prettiest girls I'd ever seen. Her name was Bethany. She was also a music student who was a remedial student teacher in the English Department for extra money. She played the flute and was a second year student in Music Therapy, a woman who had feelings for her fellow man.

She was a year older, about two inches taller, thin, had long straight blond hair, parted in the middle and flowed down to the middle of her back. She had stunning blue eyes and moved like an aberration. She had a style and elegance I've never seen before, spoke softly which gave her even more appeal, and a demeanor that made me believe she came from plenty of money. The fact that she had a job teaching remedial English made me think that possibly her family wasn't giving it to her. I wanted her to "tutor" me something fierce.

Early one morning, October 31st, I was in the basement of the music school, the ground level of a century old remodeled home, the practice area, small rooms that had pianos, music stands, quiet areas where we brushed up skills. Painted white but yellowed with time, it had old windows and doors that creaked. It had crystal doorknobs that were loose and would jiggle or didn't shut tightly, wooded floors that made me think of the young creators of sound. Students had warned the pattern into the entrances, each doorway a metaphor for entering another musician's dream. I related and spent many mornings there.

I was going over a scene for "Opera Workshop" playing "Bartolo" in the "Barber of Seville," and I felt I wouldn't get any better, not that day, and was passing one of the practice rooms on my way out. As I passed, I heard the sound of a flute and noticed Bethany practicing alone. The glimpse I caught of her through the crack of the door, sitting up straight with that silver flute to her mouth playing that slow moving, beautiful melody, made me want to quit singing and become a musical instrument. I stopped and peered in. I didn't think she could see me, but my shadow was visible through the frosted glass.

"Who is it?"

Her words startled me, and when I flinched, my head knocked against the door. Being caught, I slowly looked through the open space and said, "Hi… sorry."

Embarrassed, I felt flushed. I got caught looking when I wasn't supposed to. "Umm… I heard the music. It was really nice."

"Thank you," she said with a grin that didn't show her teeth, the corners of her smile turning upward.

"What was that?" I asked.

"Oh, something I put together as a kid. It's really nothing."

"No, no, it was pretty cool. It was pretty. It was... What's the word... belconto." and she smiled, her grin now larger filling the room.

In the awkward silence, It took all the courage I had and said, "Are you doing anything.... later? Would like to do something... later?" There was a big pause as I waited for an answer. "Later?"

"My lesson is at 1. I'll be free by 2."

"Great. I'll meet you... later...The Pub?"

"That's good," and she put the flute back to her mouth.

I slowly shut the door as to not make any noise, abruptly pushed it back open and said, "But it's Halloween."

"Yea, I know," and with a big sigh she said, "but there's nothing going on with me."

"Great!... I mean, I'm sorry you don't have anything to do, but."

She said with a chuckle, "I'll see you there... Later."

I proceeded to shut the door again, and after the doorknob made a click, I gave a very quiet "Yes!" to myself.

That afternoon I was damned excited, and we met at "The Pub," a place on campus that serves pizza and beer. Eighteen year olds could buy liquor then, so she bought a pitcher. Bethany said she didn't drink often. I poured us both a glass.

I was nervous. I didn't want to embarrass myself, but when other music students   arrived and sat at our table, it took the heat off of our one on one conversation. Together we all started to cut up and laugh.

Bethany was very attractive and knew that I was the idiot in remedial English, yet she was having fun with me, and I couldn't believe my luck. With a nervous twitch, I kept flicking my thumbnail with my index finger, and the nail started to peel off. It was weird. The pizza came, was placed on the table, and we started to eat.

Things were going well for a semi-first date. The other music students were talking about school, politics, how this world is going to hell, and how President Carter sucks or doesn't. I was talking and smiling with Bethany, and I didn't even realize I was still flicking my fingernail below the table.

In mid conversation, Bam! My fingernail popped off and went flying through the air, and as if in slow motion, landed on top her pizza. It actually hit dead center on a slice of pepperoni. I was mortified, completely and utterly mortified. She ever so coolly picked off my fingernail with her thumb and index finger, slowly extended her hand over the edge of the table, rubbed her fingers together, and it dropped to the floor. She then looked at me and gave me a half smile as to say, "Don't worry about it, this could happen to anybody," and took another bite of the same piece of pizza. In embarrassment, I put my hand to my forehead and wiped it in one slow motion down my face to my chin, like Curly on the Three Stooges. No one at the table noticed because they were busy talking.

I thought I was going to die. She then poured more beer, and nothing was said. Damn, she had class, too.

As time went on we finished the pizza, the beer was gone, and I noticed she was really having fun. She was talking a lot, touching my arm and slapping me playfully, agreeing with what I said, saying, "Yeah! You right."

She was getting drunk and acting silly, letting her hair down. I was really started to enjoy myself.

She started telling me more intimate things about herself. She had been playing the flute since she was a child. Her father was in real estate. Her mother was a doctor, and both brothers were doctors. She went to Mount Carmel Academy for girls because her best friend went there. She was talking and laughing, and I just kept smiling and smiling, feeling that this was alright.

As the afternoon went on, we playfully spoke of life's dreams, each other's destiny, even raising families. We held hands, Bethany, leaning against my shoulder looking up into my eyes and smiled. It was nice. The day was innocent, filled with a niceness that added to campus life.

All of a sudden, in the middle of the conversation, she stopped and looked directly in my eyes. She blinked hard and said, "Larry, I think I'm getting drunk."

"Well, you do look a bit tipsy."

Laughingly, with a slur, she said, "I'm not tipsy, I'm drunk, and you did it to me." She pointed at me and said playfully, "Shame on you, Larry Hyatt. I'm gonna get you for this. You've been a naughty boy, and I've been a naughty girl."

I half-smiled back.

"Hey Larr," she said and paused. "We… gotta go."

"Ok, whatever you need to do."

"I live around the corner. Can you please give me a ride? I live around the corner."

"Of course."

Getting up from the table I realized that the only street around the corner from Loyola University is Audubon Place. Audubon Place is one of the richest neighborhoods in the whole damn city. Celebrities, politicians, world leaders, they come to New Orleans to stay with friends who live on Audubon Place. These are the wealthy elite. There is a fortress at the beginning of that street that has armed guards. To enter, I would need a note from Jimmy Carter himself. This girl's family is rich. Now, I think I'm in love.

"Yeah, give me ride, Larr. I usually just walk. It's not far."

"I'll be glad to. I'm parked by the music school."

As we walked hand in hand through the campus to my car, still talking and enjoying the day, she was now swaying a bit, but not so much as to destroy the afternoon. She was quite playful actually, running around the oak trees to catch me on the other side.

When we got to my 1970 white Chevy Camaro, the car my parents bought Kellie and me and friends dubbed the White Shark because the rust on the entire front resembled teeth. I started to feel embarrassed but all was forgotten when it became awkward getting her in the car. The alcohol was taking more effect.

When I jumped in on the driver's side, I grabbed my seatbelt and pulled it across my chest. To my surprise, when I leaned toward the passenger side to click it in its buckle, she lightly kissed me on the cheek. I turned to her. We both smiled for a moment and each slowly moved to one another and kissed, ever so gently on the lips. Just long enough to close our eyes, think of the moment, and take it in. With her eyes still closed, our faces still close, she smiled at me.

"Thanks, Larry," she whispered, and then opened her eyes.

"No... thank you, Bethany. Thanks for lovely afternoon." She smiled again as she put on her seatbelt.

As I started down St. Charles Avenue, her corner came into view. You'll never miss the corner of Audubon Place. As we approached the corner, that's when her left hand reached for my shoulder and she hit me with, "I think I'm going to be sick."

I immediately b-lined for the side of the street, but before I could stop the car, she opened the door and could hear the grinding of the car door scraping the curb.

The lovely lady didn't make it. She threw up the pizza all over herself, my car, and the street. If the armed guard had been there, he would have been cleaning his uniform in the morning.

After a couple heaves and a big dry one for good luck, she lifted her head and turned toward me, her blonde hair a mess, her eyes half shut, her head tilted forward and in now a very slurred speech said, "My daddy is going to kill you."

She was beautiful. She had grace. She was funny, and she had money. But I'll be damned if "Daddy" was going to meet me today.

She said, "You better go," and GI Joe from the front of the street helped her out of the car with her arms slung over his shoulder.

As I drove away, I didn't know whether to feel happy, sad, or fear for my life. I figured I had till Monday since daddy didn't know where I lived. Then I thought hell, he could probably find me when I registered for the draft. Or worse yet, send me to the service because I got his little girl drunk like a spring break college bitch.

After I got out of that neighborhood and started to feel more secure I did think that it wasn't a bad afternoon. I did have a crush on her, and she actually went out with me. We did have fun together, but I also realized she was out of my league; "Entertainer Boy" in her family's eyes, would never measure up, would always be less smart, less rich, and less of a man who couldn't take care of their princess.

I went to my friend's house, the friend from Canada who played the drums. It was outside the garden district toward downtown. It was only 6 P.M.

Monday at "English for Idiots" I saw Bethany, and she apologized just like I knew she would, but it wasn't the same. We went too far too soon. It was the one female student I got close to my freshman year. I'll never forget her.

My Canadian friend would introduce me to another girl who would give me a different prospective on things. Her name was Alice, Alice D. After all, this was higher education.

Higher Education

At my friend's house, the Canadian drummer who said the letter "a" after each sentence as if asking a question, loved Led Zeppelin, thought the drummer John Bonham was the shit, was to be a music therapist. He even did research on American colleges and discovered Loyola was one of the best to get the degree that would make the world a better place. He came down south with an ulterior motive. He was on a mission.

Adam impressed me. For one, he wanted to soak up "the city that care forgot" and experience the plight. Being from Canada and an ambassador's son, he didn't know of inner city New Orleans or any downtrodden urban development. He moved into one of the worst parts of town and took the streetcar to class each day. I thought he was crazy. He lived next to the projects. On the days we both had class I would stop and give him a ride, being the other crazy white guy picking him up at dawn.

Things in his hood were happening all through the night. Babies were crying on porches, drunks screaming at one another. I heard gunshots bringing back memories of getting my ass kicked. Being in this neighborhood, during the holidays sent chills down my spine. If someone had said, "Merry Christmas, white boy" I would have pissed in my pants again.

He once convinced me to walk to the corner grocery. We looked liked two marshmallows in hot chocolate. Every time someone approached me I checked to see if I had on a hat and that it wasn't Martin Luther King's birthday. But Adam loved it, enjoying the vibe of the Crescent City, which he wanted to be a part of.

Adam also had a macabre streak that he said came from watching the James Bond movie "Lie and Let Die," a movie that was filmed in New Orleans. Voodoo is prevalent to the plot, and he said it had an effect on him as a kid. The drums playing in the movie at the voodoo ceremonies made him feel like something had a hold on him.

He liked New Orleans, and being French Canadian, he had a special tie to New Orleans' French heritage. I thought it being Halloween and Adam with the voodoo connection: it would be a great idea to take a ghost tour in the French Quarter. I called Jay, a friend from the neighborhood, and he also thought it would be fun to screw with our friend from the north for Halloween.

The ghost tour visits all the haunted sights in and around the French Quarter. It visits the places of beheading, family murders, voodoo ceremonies, and the elaborate cemeteries of New Orleans. The tour was guided by a very sexy woman dressed like a vampire.

When we arrived at Adam's house, he gave us a beer and breaks out this paper that looks like a cardboard drink coaster. On it, it had a picture of a dragon. He asked me, "Larry, you've done this before, eh?"

"What? Use a coaster?"

"No paper?"

"If I don't have a coaster."

He laughed at me and said, "No, man. It's acid, eh."

I'd heard of it of course. It's just up until that point in my life I'd never gone that far for a good time.

As he proceeded to break it into little pieces, my friend Jay said, "I'm willing to try it. I'll try anything once."

Being a go-along person with friends, I thought would never jeopardize my life I said, "Hell, let's do it."

The Haunted Tour started at 9 P.M. and upon arriving, things in our head were starting to get freaky. Walking through the picturesque French Quarter, we all started to talk a little faster, get a little livelier, and laugh a little bit more at nothing unparticular.

The French Quarter at Halloween is a menagerie of the wild and lurid of New Orleans. The people of the city love a chance to dress up, take pride in it, and you're more likely to find more dressed for Halloween than Mardi Gras because the tourists know what to do.

It seemed as if everyone walking the streets were in costume. It was a beautiful, clear, cool autumn night and more people wanted to be a part. We saw people dressed as ghouls, zombies, Frankenstein, and the usual vampires, people with decapitated heads, disemboweled and full of blood. We saw sexy nurses half dressed, Catholic school girls lifting their tops; we spoke to an Alice in Wonderland with her tits and ass hanging out along with her friend who was the Red Queen of Hearts. Jay was ready for her to deal him a handful right there in Jackson Square. When the tour got to Bourbon Street, Jay saw a huge fleur de lis hanging from the third floor of a hotel balcony. It was a large banner that reached all the way down to the street. The thing looked like a movie screen. It was gigantic.

He stopped, looked way up in the sky, and with his eyes wide open started yelling, "Damn! It looks like that freaking' fleur de lis is upside down! Yeah! Look at it! It's upside down, Man! Can't you see it? Wait a minute. Holy Shit! It's upside down, and it's right side up… all at the same time! That's freaking crazy, man!"

Adam started to laugh and said, "Oh, shit. Halloween is on, eh?"

We were following the tour, enjoying the weird stories of ghosts, phantoms, and old world New Orleans when things were getting stranger by the minute. That was when we lost Jay. He saw the woman dressed as Alice in Wonderland and yelled, "Alice! Alice! Alice in Wonderland! I "wonder" what you're doing tonight."

"I'm enjoying my Halloween. What are you doing?" He shouted back, "I want to Tweedeldee with your Tweedeldum."

She thought that was pretty cleaver and said with a smile, "Well then, come trick or treat with us."

I personally thought it was two guys in drag, but Jay was convinced it was women. Finally, I said, "Whatever you want them to be, Jay. It's Halloween."

He was gone.

That left Adam and I walking with the tour, which was now heading into the cemetery.

New Orleans cemeteries long ago were in the outside of the city perimeters, land dry enough to throw the dead bodies full of diseases or whatever might have killed them. So in the city, the dead were entombed in cement and at different levels. This created a "dead city' with tombs and mausoleum, memorials to the wealthy families that created the city of New Orleans.

We learned all this on our tour. Adam, into the macabre thought this was all too fascinating. Add what we had taken and the ghost stories, things started to play with our senses. We actually started looking over our shoulders to see what's going to get us. Shadows started to appear and disappear around corners of the tombs. Adam said he saw a cherub's eyes light up.

During the tour, off to the back of the cemetery, Adam noticed the name on a tomb of an old New Orleans jazz musician that he recognized, Cecile "Cowbell" Jenkins. He played the drums. He died in 1945.

"Larry, this guy played with Louis Armstrong and Jelly Roll Morton but didn't get the recognition he deserved, eh. When Cecile played, they say he "freed up" the beat. He was a big influence on jazz in New Orleans, eh."

"Why the hell did they call him "Cowbell"?

"Because he used the cowbell to syncopate a rhythm with the drums."

"No shit?"

"Freaking, eh. He made the cowbell a big part of his beat."

It sounded good to me.

The tour at the cemetery was coming to an end, but Adam wanted to hang around and let the others go so we could explore Cecile's gravesite. He was impressed with what he found and was intrigued that he had stumbled on to "Cowbell," something he knew so much about.

"Wouldn't it be the shit, Adam, if you could get Cecile's drummer vibe? You could syncopate with the cowbell. He could go all drummer shit on us."

"You know, you're right, eh. I'm here. It's now. I'm gonna' channel Cecile."

"Look!" I said, "There's a hole in the corner of the tomb. I'll give you a boost and see if you can see in."

Adam was as tall as me, and slim, so it wasn't a problem. He put his foot in my hand, grabbed a hold of the side of the tomb and pulled himself up to see.

"It's dark in there, eh, but I think I see a coffin."

"No shit? What else?"

"That's it. But, I'd like to get a better look? Push me up a little higher."

When I did, he started to chip away part of the dirty white cement of the corroded tomb.

"You see anything else?" I asked.

"Yea, something sitting on top of the coffin... I can't make it out, eh... but I think I can get to it."

Adam started to chip at the cement, enlarging the hole and he reached in.

Just then, with a sudden jerk, something grabbed and pulled his arm inside the tomb. He frantically started yelling and screaming for help. It was a blood curdling scream that scared the shit out of me. His arm was caught in the tomb, and he was screaming as if something had his hand. I moved away from the tomb in fright and Adam, scared shitless, was dangling there with his arm inside the tomb, his legs shaking wildly as if he was trying to run.

Getting up my courage, I grabbed his legs again and lifted upward, but he didn't come loose. He kept screaming and yelling for help. Then I started screaming and yelling for help. We were two grown men, yelling and screaming for help, trying to get the hell out of there.

"Larry, get me down! Get me down! Holy fuck! I can't move my fucking arm."

I kept lifting and lifting, trying to get him free, the whole time both of us yelling and screaming as if something was going to pull him inside. He was lodged in the tomb to his shoulder franticly trying to unlock his arm.

Finally, with one hard lift I thought would take off his shoulder, he came free and we both fell to the pavement. Completely shocked, breathing heavy and both stunned, we gathered what was left of ourselves. Then, I notice in his hand a "cowbell." It was old, dented, and rusted like someone had beat the thing for years. Adam and I looked at each other wide eyed and confused.

"Larry. It's a fucking cowbell, eh."

"Cecile's cowbell?"

"It ain't my fucking cowbell."

"Holy, shit… What the fuck are you going to do with it?"

"I'm not doing a god damn thing. I'm putting this son-of-a bitch back, and I'm never coming back here again. Let's get the hell out of here."

He jumped up from the pavement, crammed the cowbell back into the tomb, and we took off as fast as we could. We ran out that cemetery as fast as our stupid ass music student legs could take us. Hell, we didn't stop running until we hit Bourbon Street. Adam was in front the whole way. If something was going to get us, it only had to out run me.

In the French Quarter, exhausted, we noticed a place called The Dungeon, perfect for what was needed, a drink and a chance   to come down . My God what a Halloween that was.

Life In The City

I completed the first year as a Loyola University Music student. It was a great experience but wasn't easy, much harder than the fall. Perhaps that NOCCA teacher was right. I didn't have the discipline that I needed to crack the books. The "party gene" I got from my dad and the newfound freedom of college took a toll on studying and practicing my craft. The fraternity I joined, "I SKIPPA CLASS," didn't help either. No one makes you go to college.

I also started to have self-doubts about direction. Was I disciplined enough to enter the world of opera? Was I prepared to learn all the languages and be world renowned? I certainly wanted to. It's what I dreamed of. Did I want to act? It crossed my mind. I always wanted a career in television. I still wanted to perform; I just didn't know in what medium. I figured these were indecisions all young people have when faced with which direction they want to go. I had the summer to think about it, but I would need a summer job.

I thought about working at the fabric store. The owner's daughter was still there and still hot. I'm now eighteen years old; I could drive her to the dump. I'd just jump in the pit for her now.

Instead, I got to work for the great state of Louisiana and the only four-term Louisiana governor, Edwin Edwards. He had a program for college students in the late 70's where during the summer they'd work in state run offices. I applied for and got to work for Vocational Rehabilitation.

Vocational Rehabilitation was a government program that helped the citizens of Louisiana gain employment if they were disabled physically or emotionally, emotionally the more fun to watch. I got to meet some very strange characters. My boss told me when she hired me I was going to like it. "Larry, there is all kinds a crazy in New Orleans."

The office was located on Canal St. off the CBD and consisted of administrators, counselors, and clerical workers. Basically, it was three floors of state employed social workers. I was a gloried office boy along with two other college students. The reality being only one was needed. "Ya, gotta love Louisiana."

I would arrive to work at 8:30A.M. and take a break from 9 A.M until 9:30. Take an hour lunch at noon, come back at 1 P.M. and then take a break from 3 P.M. – 3:30. Then, quitting time was 5 P.M. Like I said, "Ya gotta love Louisiana."

People got along well in this office, and when they weren't on break, they were breaking their backs to help people get what they rightfully deserved from the state. I got a firsthand look at how less fortunate people needed help after they were in an accident or in some emotional difficulty. This place really made you appreciate what you have in life. You see, one minute these people were productive in the community paying taxes and enjoying what life has to offer, then, Wham! The rug gets pulled out from under them through no fault of their own. These people needed assistance, and we gave it to them. We had quite a few emotionally disturbed clients, so from time to time things around the office got interesting.

About 4:45 P.M. on my first Friday, I was asked to take the phones. I guess people who need assistance don't need it on Friday at quitting time. Plus, I worked for the State of Louisiana; the majority of the workers had left for the weekend. The phone rang and as instructed, I answered, "Vocational Rehabilitation, can I help you."

A very frail woman's voice on the other side said, "Who is this?"

"This is Larry," I said with a smile, and she dropped a bombshell.

"Larry, I'm going to kill myself." Like an old pro of one week on the phone, I said, "I'm sorry what did you say?"

"I'm going to kill myself."

This rattled me. My first time on the phone, and I get a suicidal women. In all my wisdom I said, "Hold on please," and franticly tried to find the hold button.

I turned to the girl at the desk behind me and said. "There's a lady on the phone that said she is going to kill herself."

The girl at the desk, Sharilla, said "Well, don't put her on hold." So I quickly picked up the phone but the woman was gone.

I turned back to Sharilla and said, "Oh, shit, I think I killed her."

Shirilla said, "Oh no, I hope she's going to be ok?"

I'm now kind of nerved at the whole thing. I realize it was stupid. This person is upset about her life, and I hung up on her to go kill herself. The phone rings again. Sharilla said, "Answer it."

It's the frail lady again and she said, "I'm going to kill myself."

"No, don't do that." I said, now an experienced suicide counselor. "Nothing is worth doing something like that."

"Is this Larry?"

"Yes, it is me. Please, if you need someone to talk to I'm here.

"I just don't like my life. I'm going to kill myself."

"No, no! Don't do that! You don't want to do that!"

I turn around and look at Sharilla, confused and trying to get some guidance. "Shrilla? What do I do? Jesus Christ! She's going to kill herself!"

That's when I heard the giggling from around the corner in the back of the office. I got up and noticed about ten people gathered around the phone all-looking my way and trying not to crack up.

The office was playing a joke. They couldn't hold it any longer, and the place went into hysterics. Everybody was laughing. I went back to the desk hung, up the phone, and just smiled and shook my head. Damn, they got me. They got me good.

Shrilla said, "Never before has someone put the suicidal woman on hold. She calls all new employees their first week and by the way, Welcome to the office."

I worked at that office for another month. There weren't enough things to do, so they sent me to the Vocational Rehabilitation on the top floor office of Charity Hospital. There were only three counselors there, even less papers to file, but this was where I worked with quadriplegics and paraplegics. This was where it got real.

As a young college student it was amazing getting to know these strong-minded people who didn't give up. I saw it in their eyes. Everything worked but their limbs and to see someone totally dependent on someone else really left a mark on me. That's when I learned that we should cherish our ability to move, to jump, and be able to reach for things when you need them; to cherish what you have.

I often looked out over the city, the jagged edges of the skyline, wondering how anyone could live without "doing." If they saw something they wanted to grasp, they couldn't pick it up. If they thought of somewhere they wanted to go, they couldn't. If they were lying on their back and wanted to roll over, they had to buzz the nurse, but wait, a quadriplegic can't reach the buzzer. They have to wait for someone who's willing to help. Don't think it can't happen to you.

Remember, some lives don't go as planned.

That summer, the New Orleans' Central Business District along with these patients were my inspiration. Enjoying the inner city, walking about in a place that before scared me, I noticed how concrete seemed to move when crowds in a rush traveled from one place to another. I wrote poems and essays about its pain and sorrow and the hero would always overcome it. I liked happy endings. I sucked as a writer and maybe still do. But, I did get to use the new vocabulary words that I learned in remedial English. I was growing and life was starting to change me.

What's The Name Of That Law Again?

I started my second year at Loyola, but the excitement of the opera that sparked me as a boy was gone. I now knew the classical music world was far too structured. I decided to take the road more traveled and would become an all around entertainer, maybe even a writer, but that would never happen.

Loyola was hard without discipline and not having anyone make me attend didn't help. I didn't study and practice constantly. Don't ever forget, my students, who have tagged along this far. If you want to be a music-major or study the arts and "Get" it, be prepared to practice constantly. Discipline will be one of your greatest assets and the music, translations, and stress, can do plenty of damage. It really started to work on my nerves.

On weekends I would go hunting with my brother and all would be quiet sitting in the duck blind waiting for the birds to fly. Crouched low and out of sight, peering just above the grass I would wait patiently in the stillness of the morning. Then, all of a sudden I could hear strange melodies and foreign languages going through my head. It was just vowels and consonants, melodies mixed together in my head, swirling, repeating again and again and again. Have you ever tried to memorize gibberish? I couldn't concentrate. It was a foreign language for Christ's sake. I didn't even know if I was memorizing correctly. And, I was failing school (Well, everything but English.)

It's sad to say, but I seemed to be tired of constantly performing and always looking for another show. But performing and being in a show was expected of me, by me.

I was in another musical at Le Petit Theater in New Orleans and that took plenty out of me. I still had piano lessons each week and had to prepare for those. My mother moved her Mardi Gras business out of the house, so I had obligations there, too. After fifteen years of performing, I was burned out. I still had the "dream." I just wasn't achieving the goal with the direction I was going. I was changing. I was growing older. Was the dream changing with me? Hell, yeah! But it doesn't die. I just had to get my act together. Damn it!

When I started to miss class, it was over. That fat lady sang. That's when I had to admit failure. Larry's Law reared its ugly head. I really dislike that law.

I was groomed by my family, friends, teachers, and directors, many different people, all of them believing in me and wanting me to make it and be noticed. This support group took me to all the music lessons, all the shows and rehearsals, not to mention the money spent, so I could get to where "I" wanted. What they expected of me was now a huge burden, and slowly it was sinking in that I had to tell Mary I can't go on.

This played on my mind like nothing I have ever experienced. It tormented me, every waking moment. Every time I had to look at music, every time I saw my grandparents, every time reality set in, I was reminded of being a failure.

I had to come clean. I had to say it out loud, "I want to drop out." I had to let everyone down, make everyone hate me, and let them know they did the wrong thing by believing in me for all those years.

That day I came home from school, found my mother in the "factory" part of the house, and told her we had to talk. I knew she was going to be upset. I remembered what happen at NOCCA, and that I let people down. Here I go again.

We went into the living room; she took a chair, and I sat on my piano bench across the room.

"I just don't like it anymore, Mom. I'm tired. I always have a show to do... I'm not even doing well, and I know you're going to flip out. Please, don't flip out... I haven't been going to school."

She nodded her head. She was thinking.

"This college thing just isn't for me, Mom. I don't know what happened. I really, really don't."

Her head was still moving, and I looked for compassion.

"I'm so very sorry, Mom."

She leaned back in her chair, folded her arms, and took a deep breath. Thinking, she raised her head and put her hand to her mouth, then to her chin. She then lowered her eyes and looked directly into mine. I was anticipating the worst.

Then, in all her wonderful "Mother Mary" wisdom said ever so eloquently, as only Mother Mary can, "Well Son…if you don't like it…don't be a pussy. Just quit."

I was floored. I fell back against the piano keys. It made that odd musical sound of all the wrong chords being played together. In my wildest dreams I never expected to hear those words. It was if God came down and saved the wretch that's me. The pressure in my chest, lifted. It was the first time I felt relieved in months. I had never felt anything so uplifting. I can't describe it. I apologized again and I told her how I didn't know this was going to happen. I also begged for forgiveness, over and over, and over again, and said, "Mom, I will make it up to you. I swear."

She very warmly said, "Look Larry, I love you. I have to. You're my son. You and I both know you have talent. I always knew you did. I also know my children and know when something is wrong. Let me tell you something I haven't told you before. When I was young, I wanted to be a seamstress. I was good at it. Everything I put a needle and thread to people loved. From there I dreamed of designing clothes, then designing clothes for the rich and famous. But I met the man I would spend the rest of my life with and things didn't work out. I had three kids, and I was on my own. That didn't stop me from wanting to be a designer. People's dreams never really die, although some people let them fade. Now, my three kids have dreams, and I want them to live theirs. I exposed Kellie to color and design. You, I pointed toward the stage, and Jimmie towards the sports field."

I wiped my eyes trying not to be a so-called pussy.

"Larry, you're gonna keep pursuing your dream. I know you will. It just might not be in a way you expected. Keep your dreams alive, and you'll be okay, son. I love you so very much." She got up and grabbed my hand and gave me a quick kiss on the forehead.

"I got to get back to work. I got a king's costume to finish, and your sister insists it can be made with an idea that refuses to cooperate. These young designers think everything can be done with a piece of fabric. She's got a lot to learn, too."

Mother Mary got to the door, turned to me, smiled and said, "Oh, by the way, this costume your sister designed, it's for Charlton Heston, the King of Bacchus this year," and she walked out the door.

I thought to myself, "I'll be damned; he's rich and famous.

Radio and a Night to Remember.

Life as I knew it had changed. For the first time I didn't have to sing, dance, act, recite, play a piano, or walk like an ostrich. I had nowhere to go, nothing to do, and Loyola University didn't care if I returned to school or not. They did want something in return for enlightening me about upper education and college girls. The priests wanted their money and like a good Catholic I had to pay for my sins.

I needed a job, but what do I do? The fabric store was now out of the question. The boss's daughter was still there but that would remain an adolescencent dream, and I didn't want to make Mardi Gras costumes.

I should have turned to my family. My brother worked alongside my uncle and cousin. They were union men. My grandfather was a charter member.

The Clerks and Checkers were men who worked alongside the Longshoremen on the Mississippi riverfront. They checked cargo from the ships that docked in New Orleans.

My family indeed wore the union label. I once had a date for a wedding and at the dinner party she went on about how unions are screwing up the workforce in America, and the Right to Work law should be implemented in all states." She wouldn't quit about her disdain for unions until my little old grandmother was about to kick her ass. Finally, Granny couldn't take it anymore and pointed her finger across the dining room table.

"How dare you come to this house and say that, missy?"
I said, "Grandma, she has a right to her opinion."

"Yes, she does, and a person should also know who they're talking to. Larry, you didn't tell her what your family does, for goodness sakes?"

Of course, Mother Mary through the years would change the end of the family sentence to for Christ's sake. I was trying to get laid, but I didn't dare tell that to Granny.

The men in my family made good money, very good money. I was amazed when I found out that there was even a Water Boy's Union. These were men who went up and down the river to the different births just to make sure everybody had enough water to drink. I thought I could be the opera singing Water Boy, make a bunch of money and pay back my student loan. This would have been the smart thing to do. But, nooooo. Larry's law was lurking. You see, I still had the dream. It doesn't die easy.

My identity was performing. I was somehow going to get paid to entertain, the next step in my plan. I'll "make it" later was my thinking. But for now, I'm a young man with no skills but to entertain and couldn't even get the paper that said I might be good at it.

One Sunday, I was out with Jay, my high school friend, cruising the lakefront. Lake Pontchatrain was where teenagers in New Orleans hung out with nothing to do on a hot afternoon. People flocked there. All day custom cars filled with young people blasting radios drove up and down the seawall. Thousands of people picnicked on blankets, played frisbee, sunbathed half dressed and partied. It was there we heard an advertisement on the radio about beingDJ and going to broadcasting school. Jay looked at me and said, "Hey, you should look into that. You studied all the other stuff."

It was true. I studied voice, piano, guitar, dance, theater, maybe now I should learn how to speak. I was longing to get back on any type of stage. My life was performing. I wasn't doing that. My identity was gone, but Loyola knew who the hell I was and where to find me. I needed a job to pay them back, so I joined the school.

Broadcasting Institute of America was a one-semester radio course that can get you an entry-level job in radio broadcasting. It was on the top floor of the WRNO Radio

Broadcasting building, now WTIX. It was located in
Metairie on the corner of Clearview Parkway and the I-1C
service road. You could see the call letters on top of the
building from the interstate. It was pretty impressive. Each
day walking into the building I pretended it was a radio
station in New York.

The number one morning show at that time was
"Wally and J.J." I thought they were the funniest guys on
the radio. It was when the morning zoo's hit the airwaves,
and they had characters and funny bits and were very
personable. I didn't ever want to be a DJ per se since I was
a singer and an actor, but being able to be articulate when I
got to the next level was blatantly needed. I related to them
as a form of show business. Plus, I figured at that time if I
could get into radio I could go from there into television.
That's what I wanted to do since I saw Johnny's Follies.

I interviewed for one of six spots in the fall semester
and was easily accepted, since I could now read out loud
and passed remedial English. The fall semester started. I
was going to be bigger than "Wally and J.J."

"Hilarious Larry in the Morning," "Lunatic Larry in
the Afternoon," "Red the Head Hyatt," were all names I
entertained. I thought "Marty Craw" was kind of cool
being its New Orleans.

I also had to pay for broadcasting school, so I found a
job at night delivering pizza for "Pizza Man, He Delivers,"
It was a neighborhood pizzeria, and they knew I was an
actor so for more money, I would wear the pizza man suit

on the neutral ground in the middle of Downman Road in front of the pizza pallor.

The suit was a cross between Superman and an Italian tablecloth, the red and white checkered one. It was hideous, but I made a deal with the inside crew that if the customer mentioned the idiot in the pizza suit, I would get a cut of the tips from the inside sales.

I did some strange things to get people to pull over. Things like stuff socks in my crotch, dance on the neutral ground and run around with my hands extended out in front of me pretending I was flying. There was a stop light on the corner. People got to stop and stare so the sock was a big hit.

No one knew who the asshole in the suit was because I had a mask and cap. They tried to get me to deliver in the suit, but I had to draw the line. I could end up at a friend's house, and they could recognize me. I knew being called Santa Claus could get your ass whipped. I would have never lived down Pizza Man. I made enough money to stay in broadcasting school. Mother Mary helped with the rest, of course.

Enrolling at that particular time was lucky. Or was it fate? You see, in my class was a second-generation broadcaster, Sal. We had met through a mutual friend, Ryan, and it was a coincidence we ran into each other again. This guy's father was a well-known announcer. People in New Orleans, Chicago, New York, and other major markets all would recognize his father's name. I was set on an inside track into the business I wanted to be a part of. What luck? I can't fail this time.

We hit it off. We were alike in the things we did, but what I really liked about this guy was that he was outrageous, over the top, an outrageous Italian who was one funny "Mo-fo." He enjoyed the hell out of being alive. He was confident and commanded a room, where as I was a safe extrovert who waited for my moments.

One night after school we met at Fat City, a strip of bars in Metairie outside New Orleans, which was a hot spot back then. He put on a big nose and glasses and walked into the place singing Italian songs like, "O' sol o mio." It grabbed everyone's attention. We would party and have fun. People loved us, but even more so, I was learning about the broadcasting industry from a guy who grew up in it. I would be invited to his house and party with politicians, Saints players, news anchors, and weather men from the different stations. These were people who could advance my career. I studied everyone and tried not to say anything too stupid for these people in the industry would be my colleagues in about ten months.

At this time, let me remind you about my voice. The voice that took so long to change, the light, airy, tenor voice, with no range. Throw in a nasal sound, and you've pretty much got my speaking voice, not the best instrument to change careers and become the next Don Pardo. But if Casey Casem sounded like he did, maybe my personality can shine. Well, that's what I hoped, so I tried to learn everything about broadcasting from these mentors.

Broadcasting school came easy. The discipline I got from Loyola told me you have to take it seriously. This time I studied. I studied hard. I practiced my speech, diction, vocabulary words, and I graduated with flying colors, Larry's Law didn't apply here, and it was now time to get our first jobs in smaller markets around New Orleans.

Sal got on very fast. He was way ahead of everyone. Months later he called and told me they had an opening at the station he worked for, so I sent a tape. I wasn't experienced enough for an afternoon slot and was passed up. I kept practicing on the weekends, whenever my teacher could let me into the building. I sent another tape to another town about two months later. That tape wasn't good enough. I persisted. I would talk to my father and see him at the Bounty, and he would tell me again, "don't say can't, and don't ever give up."

For the next six months, with the help of my dad driving me, I went back in the studio and made more tapes trying diligently and letting the teacher know I was committed. I was getting pretty discouraged when my teacher called about another job. This was for an evening shift, 6 P.M. -midnight in Houma, Louisiana, a place they called Cajun Country.

The third time was the charm.

I now needed a car, so Mother Mary gave the mechanic who lived across the street a few hundred dollars for a Chevrolet Impala. He said, "It's just the car he needs. I'll have it running in two weeks." Oh hell, but I was chasing the dream once more, and I was ecstatic. I now needed a place in Houma.

Pulling into Houma, to look for an apartment with Kellie, I wrote the first of many jokes. I saw the water tower with the word "Houma" written on it. Houma is pronounced "Home-uh." I told my sister, "Hey look Kellie, I'm moving to Houma, that's Italian for what people live in, a home-a." It was my first, and I'll never forget it.

We couldn't find an apartment and decided I would stay at a hotel until I found one, a small price to pay for my first "professional" performance. You see, I was finally getting paid for this. My curtain was to rise on a Monday, May 11th, 1981, at 6 P.M. I was on my way, my first journey outside New Orleans, my cocoon. The tight wrap was about to be peeled away.

That morning, I had plenty of mixed feelings. All kinds of questions were running through my head. Was I making the right decision? Was I giving up on music too fast, or was I just taking a different path to greatness? I knew I wasn't going to make plenty of money, but you had to start somewhere. Besides, I was going to get a day job. Maybe wait tables and eat all the scraps. I could be famous by becoming the world's first overweight starving artist.

The afternoon arrived, and it was exciting and sad at the same time. I was excited because of the new adventure. I was leaving home this time, packing up and going out to find my fortune, doing what I was destined to do. I was in good spirits because I knew I would back in about nine months. I was going to pay some dues, come back, and have a career in radio or television. I'd be back in no time with all the knowledge needed.

It was sad because I noticed Mother Mary didn't see it quite that way. She knew I was going to a small town, and she knew I had the talent to make a mark. She also had the insight to know I was on a path that could change my life. I might bypass New Orleans on to somewhere else. I also thought deep down my mother knew her baby was leaving the nest. She was finally finished raising her three kids, the three kids she raised alone, and the three kids who were her life.

Kellie still remained, but she had a life painting and designing Mardi Gras and Mary knew her only daughter, her business partner, would soon be leaving for Dallas to become a designer, the dream Kellie had for herself that my mother nurtured. Jimmie had fallen in love and was living with his girlfriend, and now he was gone and not returning.

It was 1 P.M. The car Mother Mary bought was to arrive any moment, and it was almost time for me to go. The scene in the driveway was filled with all the emotions one would expect. Oddly enough, the day was dark and gloomy. It looked like it was going to rain, but in no way did it affect me. I was buzzed with excitement, cautiously scared, and had visions of a life outside what was familiar. There were smiles, tears, laughing, and crying, as we all joked, saying goodbye over and over again. My family was a bit disappointed since I was going to a very small AM county music station that they couldn't hear. I could yell louder than the signal, and it was even more interesting since I was going from Pavarotti to Hee Haw.

Finally, the car came into view, and my mother's mouth dropped to the pavement. It was a car all right, and it was running. We could hear it from six houses away. It was an old, gray, beat up 1971 four-door Chevy Impala rusted through and through.

I am not kidding you. The car had a sideswipe down the passenger side so bad you couldn't get in either door. Both doors on the passage side were crushed shut.

So as not to destroy the mood my mother motioned politely and pulled the mechanic aside. I couldn't hear what they were saying, and I saw only their lips move. I would think he assured her that her youngest son wouldn't die on the road to stardom in a car he would need a tetanus shot to drive.

I personally didn't care what the car looked like. I was ready to find my fame. I waved goodbye. They waved back, and of course, I had to check the rear-view mirror. I reaffirmed all were full of smiles.

As I drove down the street, memories came rushing back. I passed friends' houses that I played in as a child. I passed the bushes where the Germans could never see me while playing Army man as an adolescent. I passed the fire hydrant I was told to run to and turn around to catch a pine-comb used as a football. As I got to the corner where my friends kept me out too late, talking, and thinking about what we were going to be when we grow up, I realized, I was now grown, sort of.

When I turned the corner, I suddenly started to have a panic attack. I got nervous, frightened, and the verses of "O' Come all ye Faithful" were beginning to go through my head. I was leaving my home. What the hell was I doing?

I said out loud to my boyhood stomping grounds, "Holy shit! Please Lord. Help me make it through this one. I served you as an altar-boy, and it's now time to return the favor. Please don't let me turn around! I ain't gonna turn around! I can't turn around! Tell me Lord, I'm making the right decision!"

Just then, it started to rain.

I found the knob for the windshield wipers and turned them on. Luckily they worked. The headlights would be next, and the rain gave me something else to worry about.

Tightly holding on to the steering wheel I cautiously watched the raindrops hit the glass; the wipers pushing water to the top of the car and to the seam where the windshield meets the metal. To my complete surprise, the rain went through the seam and down on my lap. The more it rained the more water came in. With every swipe of the windshield more rain came down. The whole front of the car along with my lap was now getting soaked. I was now driving through my neighborhood, and it was raining inside my car. A solid stream of water was coming down the complete length of the dashboard. My suitcases were in the back seat, and I kept turning around to make sure they weren't getting wet, the whole time franticly wondering what the hell was I suppose to do, "It's raining in my car."

That's when I started an uncontrollable laughter. I just kept laughing and laughing. Damn it, I was on my way to Houma and a beat up Chevy Impala with a sideswipe that leaks like a sieve would not hold me back. The sign from above told me I would be alright. My first day as a disc jockey had begun and that night would be one the most memorable of my life.

What a Town…What a Town

I did make it to Houma in my beat up Chevy Impala, with a sideswipe, that leaked like a sieve. With my lap now dry, I went straight to a hotel, the sleaziest I'd ever seen assuming it would be the least expensive. It was about 3 P.M. and they told me the rate was 35 dollars, but I didn't care because they had some scantily clad women in the lobby. I thought," Hey, this ain't half bad, being they are half dressed." With seventy bucks in my pocket, I thought I would go back after work at midnight and stay till morning and the next day. But I was wrong. I've never rented a hotel room before and found I would still have to leave tomorrow by noon. After noticing the "ladies", who were considered off limits I decided if I was too tired to drive back to New Orleans after work I would sleep in the car and try again later. What could hurt me sleeping in a car? The cows and the alligators? I knew nutrias couldn't climb. Or, could they?

I arrived at the radio station about 5 P.M. and I was to go on the air at 6. The anxiety was tremendous. I was scared of being me. Give me a script, and I can be anyone you want, but Larry Hyatt, he could be the buffoon, the laughed at...

The program director, who called himself Gator Joe, told me he would take the control-board for the first hour, show me the format, and if I were ready could go on at seven. At seven I was still nervous and hesitantly told him I wasn't ready. He stayed on till eight. I wanted him to do the whole shift, but I figured nervous or not, I better go ahead and give it a shot, so my first day didn't become my last. I took my seat at the control board. I was ready.

"Larry, when we open the microphone we say, "Cajun Country – KJIN," then go on with what you have to announce. Got it?"

"I got it." I could feel my face was flushed.

"You are Okay, huh? You're shaking. You, gonna be alright?"

"Yea, I'm fine. Just, umm. I'll be fine. Let's kick its ass."

I grabbed the small disc, a 45 rpm record, and placed it on the turntable. Using my thumb I picked up the arm and placed it on the edge, the beginning of the record that would become my first shot at being a professional.

I was extremely nervous, scared to death actually, inside, knowing everything was on the line. The previous song was ending. I could see it spinning, reaching the end of the vinyl. Time was running out. I had to react.

I pushed the button to start the next record. I opened the microphone and said, "Cajun Country J-K-I-N. This is Hank Williams Jr., Family Tradition." I turned off the microphone, fell back in my chair.

"That was very good," Joe said, "But we're K-J-I-N, not J-KIN." I didn't even notice I said the name of the station wrong.

My first shot at being a professional was a fuck-up. I wasn't surprised.

I then played a couple of songs, and it was time to open the "mic" again. I don't remember the name of that song nor realized what I said,

"Cajun Country, J-KIN."

"That was good, too, but we're K-J-I-N, not J-K-I-N. Get it right."

I realized that living on the East Side of the Mississippi River, the dividing line for K's and W's, I've never heard of a station with a "K." They were all "W's." He wrote K-J-I-N in big bold letters right in front my face, and it didn't happen again. I was now a professional.

The rest of the air shift was a cluster. I started sweating, really sweating. Perspiration was everywhere, my hands, under my arms, on my forehead; I had a pair of headphones with a very long cord. It kept getting wrapped around the bottom of the chair. The chair kept rolling around and pulling my head toward the floor.

"Larry, you suck." I got that phone call from some freak who said he listened to the station all the time. He talked weird with a lisp and all his "R" words started with

"W's." He said his name was "Rudy," which came out"Woo-dy."

I couldn't get him off the phone.

"C'mon, man. I wanna be on the Way-de-o"

"Look dude, I can't put you on the radio."

"C'mon, dis in Woo-dy."

"I'm sorry my man, I just can't."

"I wanna be on the way-de-o. Wet me speak to ya' boss, man."

"Look, I'm really sorry; I can't let you do that."

"I wanna speak to ya boss, man. Dis' is Woo-dy"

This guy just wouldn't let up. He was really starting to piss me off. I had my hands full, and I had to be gracious to this asshole. That's when I remembered Vocational Rehabilitation. I also realized the program director was never in the control room when "Woo-dy" was on the phone.

"Hey Rudy, is your name Joe? He started laughing. Joe was screwing with the new guy. Of course, we laughed about it and he said I was the first guy to catch him on the first night. I said, "Well, buddy, this alligator has already worn them shoes."

I finished my air-shift at midnight completely drained of energy. In one way excited as hell. In another, very tired and needed a drink. I drove around for about an hour seeing bars I really didn't want to go into by myself. I've never been to lounges I didn't know without friends. I've been beat-up before. I'm alone. It's a strange place. I kept searching trying to stay close to the radio station. At least that was familiar.

I found a place about 1:30 in the morning, called "Dena & Daphne's-The Double D's." I thought it was a strip club, but on the sign it said, "Line dancing." I remember girls doing that in high school, and if they were bare-assed doing line dancing, I would see more ham than on a Christmas Sunday.

I went in and the place was packed. Plenty people were not only line dancing, they were "country dancing." I've never been in an episode of Green Acres, but what the hell. I just heard six hours of "Cajun Country, K-J-I-N music."

I went to the bar and ordered a rum and coke. It's my drink. If it's not a beer, it's always rum and coke. That's when I turned around and noticed people were staring at me. I couldn't have looked different, right? These guys wouldn't have short hair for another ten years. Not to mention my rolled up short sleeves.

Everyone in the place had hair down his or her back, was dressed in black biker vests and faded jeans. I ignored it somewhat and kept sipping my drink, another wrong move. Thank God, I didn't use a straw.

That's when I noticed an attractive woman smiling at me from completely across the room. I turned around and looked behind me thinking she must be looking at someone else. I smiled back to be polite, nodded, and turned to the bar.

Next thing I know she's next to me. I turned to her, and before I could say a word, she grabbed my hand and pulled me to the dance floor.

I'm rather freaked out now because I'm dancing with a hot chick that just pulled me out on the dance floor. This has never happen before. She'd rubbing up against me rather seductively, but the song is in no way seductive. It does sound familiar though. It's Hank William Jr., "Family Tradition."

Now this is Okay. I mean really, really Okay. "What a town. What a town. I'm going to like this place. Shit, I'm growing old here. Right here with the women who pick "you" out of a crowd.

"Houma, I love you." My arms are now stretched wide and I'm going to hug Cajun Country. K-JIN-J-KIN, I don't care what you call it. But first, I'm going to have sex with my new friend.

We danced a few songs, slow dancing, then faster, with me stepping all over her feet trying to do something I would find out later was the two-step. I asked her loudly, over the music, "Would you like a drink?"

"Yes, I can use one!" she said, leaning over to my ear.

"Let's go to the bar. We can talk there."

At the bar she said with a perky smile, "I'll have a White Russian, I love those things. You're such a sweetie to buy me a drink and cute, too," and that's when I notice people are definitely staring. I was concerned but not wanting to be a wimp, I started making small talk about being new in town. She kept smiling saying, "a huh, a huh, a huh." A few more minutes go by.

All of a sudden this enormous guy from across the room, a gigantic, football player looking, dark complexed, bearded fat guy, in a black muscle shirt and white plastic boots no less, entered the bar, B-lines right to me, looks down at me, then at her, points his finger next to her nose and says, "I wanna to talk to you… outside!

He looks back at me with a scowl, doesn't say a word, turns around and pushes the guy behind him, like he had something to do with this, then walks out the place.

This hot girl, who I have had sex with over and over in my head, in a matter of fifteen minutes, looks at me and says like it's no big deal, "I'm really sorry. That's my husband. Let me talk to him, and I'll be right back."

My thought, "Holy Christ, this guy could break me in half, kill me, take me out with just a back hand," and not only that, "why the hell is he wearing white boots?" It doesn't matter. I don't want her to come back. She wasn't that good looking anyway. What a crazy ass town, what a crazy ass town. And now I don't want to walk outside. The son-of-a-bitch could be waiting for me.

It also crossed my mind that he could be beating the hell out of her. Honestly, I didn't want to know. I put it out of my mind, ordered another rum and coke, and thought man that was close. And, why the hell would a guy have on white plastic boots? We're in a freaking nightclub.

As time goes by I realize I'm going to be alright. That's when the lights go up. The entire place is lit. I think,

"Holy shit, this whole town is going to kick my ass." I looked at the fellow next to me.

"What's going on, dude? Why are the lights up?"

"This is Terrebonne; the bar has to close at two."

"What do you mean, close?"

"What are you, a fuckin' asshole?"

Ah, a question with a question.

I didn't answer him. Maybe he was right.

I'm from New Orleans. New Orleans has never closed in my lifetime. Not in my father's lifetime, not in my grandfather's lifetime and this is a totally new idea to me, bars that close. I've never been in one with the lights on. But now I have to leave this joint and I don't have anywhere to go.

In the bright light of this newly lit debauchery, I thought for a moment.

Well, a fine-ass chick just picked me up, and I didn't get my ass kicked. I lived through the first day of getting paid for something I've dreamed of since I was a child. I'm on my way to better things and a life of pure pleasure chasing the dream, so please, let me just get my ass back to the freakin' car while I'm still alive.

I waited until all the customers left, got in my car, and started driving. I didn't want to drive all the way to New Orleans, so I grabbed my wallet and ripped the Velcro to open it. I also didn't want to spend the 35 dollars on a hotel room and decided to find a place to park the car, get a room in the morning, and I'll have the whole day and night paid for. I started driving back to the radio station, figuring if I was going to sleep in the car I should at least stay close to something that wouldn't kick my ass.

The radio station was close to the Intracoastal Waterway, part of the canal system for ships to travel from the Gulf of Mexico to New Orleans. I was lucky enough to notice a deserted oilfield company at the end of a road along the bank of the canal. I slowly pulled down a gravel road and parked my beat up Chevy Impala with the sideswipe behind one of the buildings, and I layed down on the front seat to get some sleep. The battery still worked, so I left the radio on to drown out the crickets. I figured the nutrias and the gators couldn't get to me in the car. Then again, it wasn't sealed very tight.

KJIN softly played its Cajun-country music, and as I looked up out of my car into the stars, I starting to wind down. The sound of the AM dial gave the music a hollow sound, and I felt far away from everything I was accustomed to.

I relaxed knowing the sun would come up, and it would soon be another day, a day to chase once more.

It was an eventful first night, the first night as a "professional' entertainer. Staring out the rear window over the seat, I saw the moon shining overhead. It was full and that contentment of being under the lights I remembered as a boy came over me. I smiled but for no one to see, wondering what my friends who signed my recital book would think of me now. I wondered what my music teachers would think.

"Going to the opera, Larry?"

"No. I said I was going to the Grand Ole' Opry."

I had a pretty good feeling that things were starting out correct. I fell asleep. It didn't last long.

Radio Is Red Hot

I awoke to the loudest sound I had ever heard. An enormous sound of motors and propellers shook my car and me along with it. A rattling I thought came from a train that was barreling down. Unaware in the darkness I had parked across the canal from an airplane company. A seaplane was taking off just yards away, and it scared the living shit out me. A second plane shook me again. I caught a glimpse of it as it passed over the back of the car. The plane rocked the car so violently I heard pieces of rust fall down from the dashboard and hit the floor mats. It was daylight, and I figured it was time to get the hell out of there. I could stay at a hotel all day and night or maybe commute from New Orleans. I felt enough character was built by sleeping in a car, so I got a room at the Sugar Bowl Motel, slept till 3 P.M. and went back to work for 4.

That night at work I was on my own and made plenty mistakes, frustrated because I didn't sound like the DJ's I grew up listening to. "For Christ's sake, I have so much work to do."

The frustration did subside when I went to the office and completed the paperwork for payroll. It was three hundred and twenty-five dollars every two weeks, before taxes, but it seemed like a million, no, a billion. Finally, at twenty years old, I was making a living at entertaining.

I remember opening my first pay envelope. It made me feel like a winner. It was the first time the arts liked me back, the first time, the first kiss, and I was ready for a long wet one, a long smooch and possibly a slip of the tongue.

An element that comes into play in small market radio is groupies and to write about radio, before the internet, and not mention them would be impossible.

You see, some "enthralled radio listeners" are trying to escape from something dreadful in their lives or are absolutely screwed in the head... people you'd never want to meet. I've always said, "Working for the public would be fun if it wasn't for the people."

Some listeners actually have the papers to prove they're insane. They could take you to a cane field, dismember you with a machete, drag your appendages back to the house, cannibalize your ass, tell the cops, "I did it," with blood dripping around their mouth, and still go free. Disc jockeys are a phone call away, before the internet, we were the voices in their room.

Most were just regular people who actually just wanted to request a song and called up often; chitchat and you get to know them. It's easy for disc jockeys to get caught up in this because all DJ's have egos, and these people are stroking it. What other profession has you saying your name all through work?

The first week I was on, Sweeny called.

Sweeny was one to remember.

Being new on the air she didn't know anything about me and had plenty of questions. It was late, after 11 P.M. and with things slowed down, I, being an ambassador for the radio station, felt I should be polite. I noticed Sweeny was asking personal questions, "Where are you from?" "Are you married?" "What do you look like?"

I also noticed she was breathing heavy, and this puzzled me. I wondered if she was actually doing what I thought. So, being curious, and inquisitive, asked her in no uncertain terms, "What the hell are you doing?"

With a big, breathy sigh, she said, "I'm playing."

"You're playing?"

"Yea, I like to play."

"I'm sorry, but what are you playing with?"

Sighing bigger she said with another long, breathy tone, "My son's toy."

I'm laughing harder now and had to go for it.

"Your son's toy what?"

Out came a high-pitched moan, a woman on the edge.

"My son's… toy hammer."

Well, I lost it. I couldn't stop laughing. Is this the kind of thing I'll be doing for nine months till I get back home and become famous? This woman was having phone sex years before it swept the rest of the country.

It wasn't long before I realized you can't reach for the American dream while on the phone although it was a memorable part of the career. I do have to let you in on another, a woman who had called for weeks.

It was about 11:45 P.M., and I was getting off in about 15 minutes. She told me she was having friends over, wanted to pick me up, and bring me to her house then would get me back to the station later that morning. To her I seemed like a friend, and I guess I was. I had been talking to her for weeks. Besides, she never once said, "Play Misty" for me.

She picked me up at midnight in an old white truck. She was good looking; better than I thought she'd be. (They were never stunning) She had a slim body and a friendly face, although she looked a bit worn, I thought possibly from smoking too much or not knowing the latest make-up secrets. She didn't look threatening, blond hair, darker at the roots, and big brown eyes.

On the way to her trailer in Bayou Blue, which was miles away but still considered a part of Houma. We were traveling down Hwy 90, the truck driving along smoothly when in the darkness, a rabbit shot out in front of her truck.

Bam!

"Did you see that? I hit that rabbit!" she said.

"Yeah! You sure did. But you couldn't avoid it. Hell, the freaking thing just ran out in front of you. From the sound of the thud, I'm pretty sure it's dead."

"Oh! It's dead."

She pulled over on the side of the road, stopped, and put it in reverse.

"What are you doing?" I asked.

"I' m going back to get the rabbit."

"You hit it with the car. It's dead."

"I know. It doesn't matter how you kill 'em, as long as they're dead before you eat 'em."

"Check you out. You're going back to get that road kill."

"I'll leave it there if you want me to. I don't want to scare you."

"No. No. Umm, not at all." I said it with a big grin. "You're absolutely right. It don't matter how you kill' em."

She jumped out the truck grabbed the rabbit, and with my eyes following, returned enthusiastically. With a flop the rabbit hit the floorboard by my feet. The thing didn't have a mark on it. Not like when you shoot them and it's full of holes and blood. I was impressed.

She slammed the truck in gear and off we went to her house smiling at each other the whole way.

When we got to her trailer about six people were there. She was right. She had a party. An older guy she said was an "uncle" skinned the rabbit, but they didn't cook it. It would have been my first road kill.

The party lasted till about 5 in the morning. When the party broke up, she had a friend take me back to the station.

Listeners can be fun.

…

Amazingly, within the first two days of my new career, I had found a place to live with friends from New Orleans, a family that I knew when I was a kid. The family had moved to Houma years earlier, heard me on the radio, and called Mother Mary to see if I was that Larry Hyatt. It's a small world.

I stayed with them, extremely glad, because after the first two days I was ready to quit radio. The wife of the friend convinced me to stay.

A week into this I didn't sound like the people I grew up listening to, great talent with booming voices. I sounded high- pitched and nasal. I sounded like my voice changed yesterday. Wait a minute. It did.

I told Donna, the wife of the couple I was staying with, that I was ready to pack it up and go back to New Orleans, "forget this", and that I made the wrong decision. I said, "I should go back to singing. Radio is not my thing. I'll never make it."

Sitting across from the kitchen table she said, "Look, I keep hearing about how great an actor you are. Why don't you just pretend you're a DJ and play the part?"

Wow! It was as if a light went on. I think the house's electricity system blinked. Here I was trying to be Larry Hyatt, and as a DJ, Larry Hyatt sucked.

I used her advice the next Monday on the air, and I pretended I was Wally and J.J., Casey Casem, Wolfman Jack, even Dr. Demento. I didn't imitate them. I just studied why they sounded good, their inflections, their tone, and their use of pitch, or the way they used a dramatic pause, and how they talked with the bottom of their voices. I noticed they had a smiling quality about what they're saying, and incorporated that in my speaking voice.

I improved tenfold and learned that this was a good tool to use when in a performing situation.

Don't copy, borrow. At a mediocre level you will not sound like a pro. Donna's advice worked, and I stayed with my friends for four very fun months, rent-free. Houma was opening it arms very wide, and things were working out.

Comfort ability in someone else's house can get aggravating, and it was time to go and get an apartment. I found one in Thibodaux, Louisiana. You might have heard of the town. Jerry Reed had a song that was a huge country hit in the sixties called "Amos Moses." Amos lived "about forty-five minutes southeast of Thibodaux, Louisiana," which would have actually put him in the Gulf of Mexico if you drove fast. But hey, he gets creative license.

I was paying the deposit for the apartment when I got a call from of all people, Sal, my friend from broadcasting school. He was moving to Thibodaux for his second radio job. It was easy to figure out we should be roommates. I questioned if Thibodaux was ready for us.

Sal, my radio buddy, and I moved into Plantation Trace Apartments, where we lived a "trace" of a living. KJIN also needed a "midnight to six guy." It was the shift that followed mine. Ryan, our buddy, who introduced us no less, got the job and that put all three of us in the same apartment. Three DJ's ready to become the next Kasey Casem. (Howard Stern wasn't famous yet.)

What a party and a learning experience the next nine months would become.

To be young and alive was exhilarating.

It was radio around the clock. It was consuming. That was the focus. It was chasing a dream. You see, I, along with my friends, were young and chasing something few comprehend. We were going to be the next radio gods. To hell with Wally and J.J. We were going to be bigger. We decided to be lewd, rude, crude, totally unacceptable, and no one was going to stop us.

Ryan dubbed our apartment "The BP." It was short for bachelor pad.

Since I got the apartment, I got my own room. I paid $125.00. Sal and Ryan shared a room for 100 bucks apiece. I lost a few brain cells and didn't get any STD's so it was all-good.

I got the scars to prove it when Sal fixed his world famous grilled cheese sandwiches.

One night after work, Sal mentioned his famous grilled cheese. Famous because he put butter on the outside of the bread before he grilled them. Don't tell anyone it's his secret.

I was rushing to get something to drink and grabbed a drinking glass out of the cabinet. As I was getting another for Sal, I moved my hand quickly across the sink and a glass sitting on the counter collided with the glass in my hand and shattered.

It felt like an explosion. A huge piece of glass went under the skin in my hand and the blood starting flowing, a thick stream, shooting out over the sink and onto the wall. The red blood on the "apartment white," on the kitchen wall made it look like a scene from the movie   "Saw." Sal, in the other room, came running. My first thought was to go to the garbage can.

Sal yelled, "No! Put your hand in the sink!" so I tried to stop it there, but the blood kept flowing and flowing. Thoughts were now moving fast, and since that wasn't working, the blood, now everywhere, was starting to freak me out. I ran into the bathroom leaving a trail of red blood through the hallway.

When I finally stopped the bleeding, about twenty minutes later, we both decided I should go to the hospital to get some stitches. First, we ate the grill cheese sandwiches. After all, they were famous.

At Thibodaux General I was feeling much better. I had eaten the most famous grilled cheese sandwich in the world, and Sal and I actually started having a lot of fun in the emergency room by talking to the nurses, joking with the doctors, and laughing with the other patients.

Sal was having a ball. He was working the sick beds.

He brought along his big nose and glasses, and was singing in a big Italian voice, "Stick with Al Scramusa and you'll never be a loser, 1826 North Broad." It was a reference to a local crawfish place that had a big nosed Italian in their television commercials. He had everyone laughing in sick bay. Remember, he wasn't the one bleeding.

We were two comedians with a whole new audience and we loved it. They stitched me up. Sal got a patient's telephone number, and we were on our way.

As we were leaving, saying goodbye to the night shift, who actually walked us to the door since we were such a big hit, well, either that or they were making sure we didn't come back, walking toward the exit, I looked through the sliding glass door and into the lit parking lot. That's when I noticed "her."

She was stunning. She was blonde, blue eyed, athletic and shapely, my height, but that 80's big hair made her look six feet tall. The doctors had given me medication; it made me think I was dreaming. I wasn't.

The hospital door slid open, and as I walked through she walked past.

Our eyes met momentarily. She gave me a big smile. Never before had a woman that beautiful smiled at me.

I turned around a little confused to get another look, and to my amazement, she had turned around, too. I smiled. She smiled again, and turned back around to walk away down a hospital hall that seemed to say goodbye. Everything was in slow motion. She had on a tight skirt and looked even better walking out of my life.

I was still looking backward when, Bam! I ran into the sliding glass door and smacked my face. I'm glad I didn't put my hand up, or it would have broken the stitches.

Sal said, "Holy Mary, Mother of God, Larry, did you see that?"

"The door or the girl?"

I started to feel the throbbing in my hand, and in pain said, "Are you kidding? No one has ever smiled at me like that."

"She was smiling at you, my boy. Go get that."

"Smiling is one thing. Talking to me is something else and damn my hand hurts."

"Shit, that girl likes you, man. Go dude."

To be totally honest at this time in my life, Larry Hyatt couldn't get laid in a whorehouse with a wad of hundreds, so I really didn't want to follow her and get turned down again. But the look in Sal's eyes, the medication, and the throbbing hand made me say, "What the hell?"

I went back into the hospital, hurried down the hall, and turned in the direction she was going. I didn't see her, so I went down the next hall. She wasn't there either, and I took one more chance down another hall but was too late. She was gone. I got back to Sal, and he could tell I didn't find her. He was over it.

It was about 1:30 A.M. and the clubs were closing, so we went to a little bar on the Nicholls State campus. Sal ordered a "scotch and water."

I told him, "That's what my brother, my dad, and my uncle drink, but I can't drink scotch to save my soul. It's an Irish thing or something, but I don't think I'll ever like that shit. I hate scotch."

"No, you have to develop a taste for it" he said.

"No. It's pretty disgusting."

"I'm telling you, scotch is good. We should go see your dad when we go home for the weekend."

"You know, you're right." I ordered what I always drink, rum and coke.

The next morning I got up, jumped in the Impala, and drove to Houma to pick up Ryan. It was raining, so I put a plastic garbage bag over my lap as to not get my pants wet. I also bought an umbrella and would keep it in the back seat. Ryan would open it in the car when it rained just to screw with me. I had expenses now so fixing my car was on the back burner, and calling Mother Mary for money and admitting I couldn't make it on my own was completely out of the question. Besides, the car only leaked when it rained.

I got to the station about 8 A.M. Ryan was in a meeting with some new sales people, so I waited with Gator Joe in his office and explained why I had a bandage on my hand. There was a knock on the office door.

The station manager stuck his head in and said, "Excuse me, this will only take a minute. This is Katie, a new sales person who starts next week. I just wanted to introduce her to everybody."

He moved out the way, and the figure moved into the office. I was stunned. It was the girl from the hospital. My bandaged finger started to throb as the station manager said in a slow southern drawl, "This is Gator Joe, our program director."

Katie extended her arm, and Joe shook her hand.

"And this is Larry Hyatt, one of the disc jockeys."

Our eyes met and we both half smiled.

She said, "Wow, what a coincidence."

"It certainly is," was my reply, which came out in a high-pitched voice like Curly from the Three Stooges. I cleared my throat and said in a lower voice, "It's nice to meet you."

My mind was racing, and I was trying to act natural as they all spoke to one another. They turned to leave, and Katie turned back toward us and said, "It was very nice meeting you Gator. Larry, what time do you go on the air?"

"Six. No, four. No, six. I come to work at four."

"Oh good, I'll listen this evening," and she walked away.

All I could do was shake my head and feel like an idiot.

"She's pretty good-looking," Joe said.

"You have no idea. I saw her last night at the hospital when I got these stitches. That's what she meant by a coincidence. I oughta ask her out."

"That wouldn't be a good idea we have a no-dating policy."

"You're kidding me."

"Yea, the company frowns on it."

I thought, "Oh great. This woman smiles at me. I think she's gone forever then falls in my lap and I can't do anything about it."

Joe held up his hands and said, "I don't know anything." Then turns away as if to say "What I don't know won't hurt me."

I took Ryan back home and told him the story. It was raining, and as I spoke, I felt like a cab driver talking to a fare in the back seat. The umbrella was open. He looked like Mary Poppins trying to fly out of a taxi.

Sal was still up from the night out, and I told him the girl at the hospital is now a fellow employee who can only be a friend. He said. "Hey, if she's in striking distance, don't let anyone know you're a cobra."

"You're damn right," I said. "I'm a king cobra!"

"Hit her with your python baby!" he shot back.

"I'm gonna rattle that shit!"

"For goodness snake, you are the man! He grabbed my shoulders and shook them. "Crawl on your belly like reptile!"

We looked at each other for a moment.

"Ummm… I'm out," I said, "I ain't got nothing."

"Yeah, me either. Larr, want something to eat?

"Yeah, I'm kinda hungry."

"Grilled cheese?"

"Fuckin' right."

Umm, uh, umm, uh, ummm

Katie and I had been working together for about six months. We could tell we liked one another. She was older, thirty-two, and fun to talk to, (A sharp contrast to my inexperienced twenty-years old.) I would eventually find out she moved from New Mexico because she was going through a bad breakup and applied for the job when she read in a trade magazine our station needed an experienced sales person. It was her aunt who was in the hospital that first night I saw her.

I had a huge crush on Katie, but with company policy, we just stayed friends. Me, never wanting to make waves, finding the chance to perform, and get paid for it far outweighing lust. I worked hard to get to a professional level and to lose this like other chances was not what I wanted.

I was promoted to the midday shift during this time. It was a feather in my cap, and I was given the show called "The Swap Shop," the most popular show in town. This was a talk show. Thousands of people listened each weekday to people who called with items to buy, sell, or swap.

Plenty of the DJ's thought the show was a joke, corny, beneath them, but like everything pertaining to performing, I took it very seriously. To me, for the first time I had my own talk show.

The show let me open up and allowed my personality to come through. I wasn't just joking about songs. "The Swap Shop with Larry Hyatt" was talking one to one with people who made me feel good. I wanted them to feel good, too. As a performer I always felt I was there to enhance what people already enjoyed, be it the music, the theatre, or radio. I thought doing it that way would take the fear from that black space that beaconed. "Oh Come all ye' Faithful" was always the next performance away.

During the Swap Shop I'd say something funny about cars, boats, trucks, people selling dogs, cats, used toilets, even dentures. Cajuns are funny on their own. All I had to do was tweak it. It was also the first taste at being a local celebrity. I was on the ground running, and the dream seemed "so" obtainable.

One Friday afternoon, I was about to get off the air at 2 P.M. and was on the speakerphone with a girl I had a date with for that night. I was calling to see if we were still on for the evening. Kellie had taught me that.

"I'm so sorry, Larry. I can't make it after all."

"Oh no. Everything, alright?"

"Yea, but I can't go out tonight because my family is doing the…"

I don't remember what the hell she said because Katie had walked in the control room and sat down during the conversation.

I remember thinking, "This is great. This woman is busting my ass and in walks Katie. I hung up the phone and said to the room. "Well, that sucks."

"What's up?"

"Oh, nothing."

"No. What?"

"My date just got canceled."

"Yeah, that does suck."

Now, till this day I don't know why I said the next words or what made it come out of my mouth. It just happened. I looked at Katie and said, "So, what are you doing tonight?"

"Actually nothing. Why?"

"Well… let's go do something."

"I'd love to."

The only sounds I could utter was, "um uh, um, I um, ma, huh?"

She said, "Look, lets meet at 8:00 at Blues Two for a couple of drinks and maybe dinner from there. I'm really ready to have a good time. Sounds good."

I said, "Ah, umm, uh, um, ma, huh?" She got up and left.

I was dumbstruck. I couldn't believe my luck. I jumped up, cranked the music, and started dancing around the room, pointing my fingers in the air. I started singing the songs and the guy in the next room starting beating on the glass because I was making too much noise.

Then it hit me. What the hell am I doing? I could lose my job. She could lose her job. Damn! I don't know what to do. We'll just have to keep this quiet because I'm going. I'm going. I'm going. I'm going. I was dressed and left my house at 7 P.M.

Growing up in New Orleans, it took a long time to get to where I was going. In Houma you didn't have to leave early to get anywhere. At that time I would leave entirely too early to get to someone's house, and since I was always too early, I would know every bush and shrub in their neighborhood before I should actually go to the door. Sometimes I felt like a stalker.

I drove around Blues Two for about an hour and showed up about 10 minutes late. I didn't want to seem anxious.

Katie was sitting at the bar. Thrilled she showed, I said with a smile, "Hey stranger."

"Now look, Larry, we have to make a pact and not tell anyone because you know how office politics can get difficult. I mean nothing's going on, right?"

"Hey, I just happened to come by the same night you did. What a coincidence."

"That's right. We're just two employees... who ran into each other."

"I'm good with that... just friends." And we shook hands. That silly friend hand shake you use when you make a pact.

Katie would never let our jobs be in jeopardy, and I certainly wouldn't jeopardize hers. She was a class act, and it made me like her even more. She ordered a beer, and I ordered a rum and coke. I wanted to relax a bit and knew a shot would do it, so I ordered an "Italian Valium." My brother and I would drink them at my father's place. It's Amaretto and gin floated on the top with the back end of a spoon. We watched the bartender fix them, and Katie talked about different drinks and the interesting ways to make them. We drank, loosened up: Aware of our mutual affection but knowing it would stop there.

We talked to the people at the bar, and they recognized my name from the radio. They listened to the swap shop and liked to hear people sell all the different crazy things. We decided we weren't hungry and blew off dinner. The DJ showed up, and the music got louder.

The Blues Two had a light up dance floor like the one in the movie "Saturday Night Fever." It was the eighties but the seventies in Houma were still in vogue. We were having a great time dancing on that light up dance floor, drinking and laughing.

It went on for hours. She was laughing at my jokes, enjoying hearing about my family who made the Mardi Gras costumes, my sister the artist, and my father the bar owner. She mentioned we should to go to New Orleans and party one day, maybe even on Mardi Gras. "It doesn't cost you a thing to drink when your father owns a bar," I said.

It was about 11 P.M. when she said, "Come on, "Larr", let's get out of here."

We jumped in her car and went to another place, then another. Everywhere we went we had fun dancing and laughing. What a night. What a night.

It was about 2 A.M. and Houma was closing down. At that time Lafourche parish stayed open all night long. So off we went, back to Blues Two.

We were half the way there when she said, "I don't feel like dancing anymore. What would you like to do?"

"I really don't care what we do. I'm having a great time."

The next thing she said seemed like a line from an old movie. I think it is. The clichéd line that says I want you.

"Well, Larr, your place or mine?"

All I could say was, "Um, uh, um, ma, uh… huh?"

"Let's go to mine. It's closer. I'll bring you back to your car in the morning."

So I said, "Oh, ah, um, ma, uh….Huh?" She took that as a yes.

I was nervous. I haven't had much experience with this type of thing, and I now know without a shadow of a doubt, I think I'm getting naked with the woman whom I've wanted for months, dreamed of since the moment I saw her, and had to work every day along side but ignore. I'm thinking, "Larry, don't embarrass yourself, not tonight."

We turned into her apartment complex, a very expensive group of new townhouses that was just built, and I'm thinking I need a rum and coke, really bad.

She parks the car, and we walk past trees and shrubs that I'm trying to memorize in case she kicks me out for wasting her time. We get to her door, and she hands me the key. I put the key in the door, and she grabs my ass, a big hand full and shakes it. All I could say was, "Oh, ah, um, uh, huh?"

She laughed and said, "Get inside, now."

I said, "Oh shit, ah, um, uh um…huh?"

She told me to have a seat, and I sat on the couch as she walked into the kitchen. I could see her through the space that was above the stove and below the cabinet. A small square but big enough to see her smile and shoulders. She asked, "Would you like a drink?"

I said, "Uh huh!"

She opened the cabinet, and while checking out its contents, she asked loud enough for me to hear, "What do you drink?"

I managed to say a word, the drink I always drink, "Rum!"

Looking into the cabinet, she yelled back, "All I got is scotch!"

She then stuck that beautiful smile around the corner of the cabinet and asked, "Do you drink scotch?"

Well, my friend. I have been drinking scotch and water ever since that fateful night with Katie. I love the stuff. It's my drink. Ask any of my friends.

That night that young man learned plenty about love, life, virtue, waiting for the big payoff, not kissing and telling, that a date can change at a moment's notice, the love of older women, and the delicious taste of twelve year old scotch.

The things we did started slow then became fast, then forceful, frantic, freaky, and unforgettable. It stopped, started again, and became a night (and morning) etched into my memory. I especially remember big fluffy pillows.

We went out two more times and did pretty much the same thing without the impact of delirium. Katie then went back to New Mexico to her boyfriend. Me, I kept on trying to be the best announcer I could and chase the dream that was still very much alive.

In time I was going to meet the first woman I lived with. She was older, too. Just how I liked 'em and had young kids just like my Mother Mary. She would even end up co-hosting on the swap shop. I would have someone to take for the ride.

Big Fish In a Small Pond

Sal and Ryan would go back to New Orleans. Ryan missed his girlfriend who would become his wife, and Sal was far too talented to stay in a small market. Both back home and doing well, I was very proud of them. Ryan worked with a New Orleans icon from the 70's, while Sal went on to the market leaders. He called himself, "The Big Stromboli." Now that's Italian. He and his family would go on to tremendous things in the radio broadcasting industry.

We had some great bachelor memories.

One was when the landlady sprayed the apartment for roaches. Never before have I seen so many tiny little bugs and on the white paint of the BP, I thought, "Who knew they could hide like that." Minutes after the exterminator sprayed the cracks in the wall, the landlady ran out yelling. I could have sworn three early 20-somethings were clean, really.

Another night a friend came by extremely drunk, walked through the door, and picked up my cowboy boot sitting on the floor by the sofa. I followed him into the kitchen wondering in disbelief why he wanted it. In the kitchen he pulled out his dick and tried to piss in it. I said, "Hey, give me back my boot." He looked at me through blood shot eyes, handed me my boot, staggered out of the kitchen and into Sal and Ryan's bedroom, grabbed a plastic clothes hamper, the ones with the squares in it, walked outside into the middle of the courtyard and peed in there. I let him.

But most of all what I remember was the friendship. We were three twenty-something's pursuing our dream, living entirely on desire and plenty of heart, and didn't have two nickels to rub together but, the whole world was there for the taking. It was up to us and we had no doubt we were going to be extremely popular national air personalities. I was trying anyway, chasing the dream I always had. I didn't know it at the time, but the only thing certain was change.

With my friends back home, I got a little house on the Intracoastal Canal up the street from where I spent my first night in Houma. The first two mornings that damn plane woke me up. The third morning and every morning after that I slept like a baby.

Cruising along playing the local celebrity doing the Swap Shop and feeling like I was actually getting somewhere, I was becoming a bigger fish in a small pond. The money wasn't good, and Mother Mary would remind me of it, but she knew I was happy. I think she just didn't want me to work as hard as she had to. It was two years into my stint in Houma when Veronica was hired as a receptionist.

Veronica was 11 years older than me, but hey, I liked older women. They held my interest, and I thought they were more attractive than women my age which was now the ripe old age of twenty-two. Veronica had a lot of spunk. She was always laughing and always had fun things to say. She was a "sister chick," more of a Mary Ann than a Ginger, easy going, and made me feel talented. She had three daughters aged 6, 10 and 12. It didn't scare me away. My mother raised three kids, and I admired the type. I wanted to ask her out. Actually, I just wanted to do her.

Interestingly enough, the general manager started dating a sales person and that policy about in office dating went by the wayside. Veronica and I, becoming friends and office mates, pushed me to up the ante.

"Hey, V, there's a wedding this weekend in New Orleans. My high school friend is getting married. Would you like to go?"

"I'd love to but I got the kids and… blah, blah, blah, blah, blah."

"Well, that's Okay; we'll do something when you can get away."

The next week I asked again.

"Hey, V, if you don't have any plans for the weekend and you can get someone to watch the kids, we can do something. Maybe go to dinner?"

"I'd love to, but one of the kids got his hand caught in the car door, and I'll be busy this weekend and …blah, blah, blah, blah, blah."

"That's okay, maybe some other time."

The next week I got, "I'm really sorry, but one of the kids got in poison ivy and I really have to take care of him."

"That's not very good, maybe some other time?"

I pretty much gave up, and then she asked if I would like to come over for dinner. She must have been ovulating. I was rather surprised and said, "I'd love to."

"The final episode of MASH is coming on, Larr. Why don't you come over and I'll cook and watch the show."

"Cool, one of my favorite shows. That'll work."

I went to dinner at Veronica's that night, watched the final episode of MASH, the kids went to bed, and I stayed for two and a half years. "V" cooked one mean rump roast. Va Va Voom!

I actually woke up the next morning, left through the back door, and reentered the house through the front door pretending to just arrive that morning. That way the girls wouldn't know I stayed all night with their mother. I did that for about two weeks. Six months later we moved to our own place, kids and all.

The first taste of family life was enlightening. I was in love with V and loved the girls, and we both were good for one another. Mother Mary was rather freaked out with her being so much older than me, but if I loved this woman, my family would love her too. And they did.

Living with V made it possible for the first time in my life to have discretionary income. With both of our salaries we did well. In time we had both gotten a raise. Hers came when she was moved from the front desk into the computer department, and it was at this time she thought we should put the extra money we had to good use to upgrade my life. She wanted to put both of our checks in the same account so I said, "fine." Then "we" bought a new washer and dryer, new refrigerator and microwave, all to be paid for at a later date. The television she said, "Was good enough for now."

Life was good. I was chasing the dream, enjoying a house filled with kids and homework, picnics, family fun, and never before, really cool home appliances.

Everyone at work saw how great we got along. So, the general manager got the idea of putting her on the air with me while on the Swap Shop. Veronica thought it was a great idea, a fantastic idea; she loved it. I really didn't have a choice because I felt it was a done deal before they even told me. I really didn't care though. I loved her, so let's be a team.

The Swap Shop aired Monday through Friday from 10AM-11AM and for the first 15 minutes I would read letters that were mailed in. The rest of the show I took phone calls. The plan was for Veronica to read letters along with me. It sounded good on paper.

She wanted a different name, a handle, and I felt it should have three syllables in the first name and one in the last to go along with "Larry Hyatt and na-na-na.... na." We came up with Monica Wells. "Monica" because it was close to Veronica; we used "Wells" because we could play on the name- "Alls wells", "The wells don't hold water", "you're nothing but a hole… in the ground." And so on. I came up with Wells along with my friend who tried to piss in my boot.

I'd like to say that putting Veronica on the air with me was a good idea, but I can't. It was not a good idea. It was brilliant. I would read a letter about an item someone had to sell and then she would read an item. I would say something extremely witty. She would then top it.

I would write the jokes the night before and use them during the next day's show. I would put some funny zingers in for her to say and send it back to me. She was pretty quick witted herself so it worked much more than it didn't and we had a great sexual tension on the air.

Our exchanges went like this.

If a kid's toy was for sale, I might say, "I was the type of kid my mother told me not to play with."

"Then I guess you had to play with yourself."

"I did everyday."

"I bet you did."

"What do you have for sale?"

I patterned the banter after James Garner and Mariette Hartley who were doing Polaroid commercials back in the 70's. They used fast wit with a battle of the sexes vibe. It was great radio.

The show went huge. We were a hit. They raised the commercial rates and never before did it sell so well. It was always sold out.

"The KJIN Swap Shop with Larry Hyatt and Monica Wells" kicked ass. We started taking listeners on road trips. The Urban Cowboy craze was big, so we took two Greyhounds with listeners to "Gilley's" in Houston for New Years Eve. We went on beach trips to Florida, but the thing that thrilled me the most was when the station across town canceled their Swap Shop. The Swap Shop in Thibodaux, our competitor, went on the air the same time we did. They couldn't get callers anymore. They dropped it to a half an hour, then dropped it completely, and started playing music.

This is what thrilled me the most. This was the first time I really knew I had some talent. These listeners didn't know me. They didn't listen out of obligation or because they were friends invited to my recital or family who had to amuse the family idiot. They enjoyed what I had to offer. I felt ten feet tall. Yes, life was good. The appliances were paid for, and I was chasing the dream. Then our age caught up with us.

I was talking to the oldest daughter one afternoon and she asked about going to get her driver's license and that she wanted to get a car. It hit me. This is Veronica's kid. She deserves her driver's license and a car. Mother Mary got me a car (even though it was a Chevy Impala with a sideswipe.) I really wanted to do this for this kid and felt she deserved it. She was a good kid, and eventually, two more children would be asking, but I didn't have plenty of money and with a household of three growing girls, it would become even more difficult as time went on.

Added to this was the fact that with the new family life of wonderful Cajun cooking and sleeping better at night, I gained weight. By coincidence a new company in town called "Nutri-System," asked me to go on their diet and then talk about my weight loss on the air. In fact, I was the first of many local celebrities to go on Nutri-System in the area.

Well, it worked for me, too. I lost twenty-five pounds, and with that came a new confidence that I've never experienced before. The weight loss, the new confidence, the girl's growing, and our eleven-year difference in age led me to question what I was doing. I'm twenty-five years old, living with a woman thirty-six, and her three soon to be teenage girls. This could put a kink in the "chasing the dream" hose. But, I was happy.

But, I was chasing the dream.

But, I was happy.

But, I was chasing the dream.

I couldn't see myself not "making it" or at least continuing to try so I decided to end the relationship. It was a hard decision. I didn't want to hurt anyone. I'd gotten close to these girls and their mother, and I'd shared their thoughts and dreams. Being a product of divorce, I didn't want to be a man who gives up. I didn't want to be my dad. I didn't want to be a failure at this.

More decisions needed to be made. I was going to be moved to a bigger FM station that was going to be playing Top 40 music. I would be getting more money, and I would have a morning show. The hottest place in radio, a direction I wanted to go. I had to move on.

There was a good friend at work, Geoff, who I admired a lot. He was funny, really funny. He was extremely funny. He came up with jokes out of nowhere. He could read a street sign and come up with ten one liners. He was ten years older, had a television background, and had moved around to different radio stations. We got along great at work.

Geoff, along with Veronica and I, liked to laugh and cut up. We were both in a play that V had directed at the local theater. He had become a good friend of Veronica's and mine.

Geoff was a character, too. One night he studied his lines at a local happy hour and caught too much of a buzz before a rehearsal. He picketed the Little Theatre. He walked up and down the downtown street with a sign that said "unfair" when they told him he couldn't smoke in the building. He would do crazy things like that to make a point.

Geoff also had a house with a spare bedroom. I asked him if he would rent it to me for a while, until I could get on my feet and get my own place. It would only be for a short time. He said sure. So, in a very emotional goodbye, I closed the chapter in my life with Veronica and moved into Geoff's spare room, a bit leery because the picketing incident swept the local theatre community, a community I was now a part of, enjoyed, and didn't want to lose. I cared what people thought of me back then. To this day, Mother Mary apologies for making me worry about people's opinion of me, and to this day I tell her, "You fucking bitch. Mother, look what you did to me." (Just kidding.) I told her, "I'm glad someone looked out for my character."

My friendship with Geoff would become a long and lasting one. He became my mentor and my trusted friend. A person sent down to lead me farther on my path, a true and loving brother, and Veronica? Don't go away. You're going to be amazed at what happens to her.

My Mentor

Geoffrey's forte was writing. He wasn't a "front" guy. I was a "front" guy that couldn't spell his name. (Oh, wait. I did learn that in remedial English.)

Together we would end up performing on radio, in television, and in stand-up comedy. We wrote plays for non-profits that made plenty of money but not for us. We were happy, happy to be in the business, happy to have a chance to do what we loved. We produced a comedy night at a Houma hotel where we would write and perform fake dating games and give the contestants the funny questions *and* the funny answers to enhance the show. Don't ever leave a reality show to reality. They don't do it today, and we didn't back then. Remember students, if you can think of it, you can produce it, and we had one hell of a time since our personalities were the same.

Geoff had great stories, and he wanted to write my morning show with me. I needed help with this new promotion.

When Veronica and I were together, I always wrote the Swap Shop the day before. That way everything was complete when I awoke to go to work. I slept better knowing tomorrow's show was ready and waiting for me. Geoff, on the other hand, liked to get his drinking done after work at happy hour and do his writing in the morning. Since he was the funny one and much better at it, I said, "Its five o'clock somewhere."

Here is how we started our day. At 4 o'clock in the morning we would both get up and go to the typewriter. We didn't have a computer. It was a manual Underwood typewriter that we bought second hand. Geoff saw it at an antique store, and the owner told him it would be ten dollars.

"Look, I do want this typewriter, but it's broken."

"No, it works," the guy said. "See?" And he started typing on the page.

"Yeah, it types but only capitol letters. Plus, it skips to every other line."

"Yeah, I guess you're right. Give me two bucks."

Walking out with the typewriter, Geoff said through the side of his mouth, "Radio copy is printed in caps and on every other line. We just saved eight bucks." When we laughed about it all the way home I knew we had a long lasting friendship.

We then stole a full box of old yellow Teletype paper from the radio station. Not really stole. Teletype machines were now computerized and used computer paper, and we knew no one one would miss it in the supply cabinet. One end of the yellow paper is on the top of the box. The other end is on the bottom. It must have been two miles long. We could chase this dream for millennia.

Each morning I would get up and go through the newspapers, stories from the news-wire, and the jokes we wrote on napkins that we heard people say at happy hour the day before. You see, when Geoff got off at 4 P.M. we would go to a happy hour at our local hang out called the Key Club. In the morning I would read the stories to Geoff, and he would start typing.

Going through the napkins from the night before and reading things we said to one another through the evening was very enlightening. I read things like, "White on rice is nice." Both of us would look at each other and wonder what the hell was funny about that. Last night drinking at the Key Club it had everyone laughing.

When we pieced together at least ten jokes, I needed 8, (two were funny.) He'd rip the paper and hand it to me. I would then take a shower and get to the station for 5:30 and record the characters for my show.

I had many. A singing weather guy who would sing the weather in opera, a guy who did sports who we called the "Coach" who sounded like Louie from "Taxi", a gay guy, who did celebrity news, who Geoff said should *back* out the closet each morning to the tune of "Hurray for Hollywood," just to name a few.

Geoff would go back to sleep until about 8 A.M. then go to work for 9 A.M. and host the midday show. I got off at 2 P.M. and would go home take a nap and get ready to start writing at happy hour at 4 PM.

This went on as I laughed and learned to take a subject, put it in the middle of the circle, and go all around until you got the joke you were looking for. It was comedy brainstorming.

My Swap Shop was very tame. It was G rated, and my humor never upset anyone. I would read one liner books and *Reader's Digest* and repeat the comedy from them.

Today with the Internet there is an abundance of material. Back then you had to come up with this shit yourself. It worked for the Swap Shop; the listeners who scoured the classified, but it wouldn't work on top 40 Radio with disc-jockeys getting more and more outrageous. The morning shows were coming of age, and Geoff had to push the envelope.

At this time, the small town of Houma and the powers that be weren't ready for people to go on their airways and blast them about the way the city council, school board, hospital, or politicians conducted themselves. Geoff let them have it. I didn't think we were being mean. I assumed we were making jokes. Besides we got our material from the news, so it was a fact, with of course, our *observation*.

Geoff taught me you could get away with hitting the establishment but never make fun of the masses. They are our friends. I also learned the hard way not to make fun of establishments if they are our best clients. Don't bite the hand that feeds you.

On the front page of the *Houma Daily Courier*, which because it didn't come out on Saturday, I referred to as the

"Houma Daily, except Saturday Courier," had a headline
and picture of a small robot that was very popular in the
local hospital's pediatrics department. The little robot
would deliver dinners to the kids. Meanwhile, there was a
rumor going around that a doctor and nurse were caught in
"X-ray" in a compromising position. They were tucked
away in one of the corners, going at it so furiously on a
stretcher that they slammed into the X-ray machine. It
created an incident they couldn't get out of.

Our joke was, "The little robot that was in pediatrics is
a great addition, but the hospital administration said it has
to go. It was caught in X-ray with a respiratory machine."

If you didn't know the rumor, you just thought it was a
silly joke. If you *heard* the rumor, you got the joke.
Back then it was a huge mistake.

The head of the hospital actually walked to the station
from down the street. I got called in to the office and
almost lost my job. I had to write the first of a few letters
apologizing.

Other jocks said they wouldn't apologize for what they
said, but if I offended someone, I didn't mind saying I'm
sorry. By then it was so hard to "cut" funny. Plus, it was
just a joke.

I was once chewed out over the phone by a school
board member for saying this on the air that Geoff wrote. "I
was passing Terrebonne High School yesterday after work
and saw they are building a huge parking lot for the
students. Man, I hope they don't start cutting programs, so
the kids can have a paved parking lot. But I guess it a good

thing. Now at Terrebonne High they'll teach beginners parking, advanced parking, and sex education."

Back then it was a bad move on my part. Public officials just weren't used to being questioned about their actions. A school-board member called and was furious.

"Who the hell do you think you are?"

"What do you mean, sir?"

"You know what I mean! How dare you say that to the people out in the public? Where did you get that information, son?"

"Actually, I was passing the school and saw them putting down the concrete. They are building a parking lot, right? Hold on please," and I put the phone down.

I could still hear him yelling through the receiver. I actually ended up voting for this guy when I lived in his district.

Geoff and I were having the time of our lives. One of the more memorable things we'd do was wake up early on Saturdays at dawn, grab a six-pack of beer, a pack of Marlboro, an ink pen and paper, and jump into his white '62 Cadillac convertible, and head down the bayou. Any bayou, it didn't matter.

With the top down, the sun would come up, the radio played and we'd make jokes that got funnier the farther south we drove. Geoff would finish his cigarettes and enjoy flicking the cigarette butts straight up, letting the wind take them.

"Geoff, you ought to give up the damn things, man. They're not good for you."

Speaking over the wind in our ears, he said, "Don't worry about it, I don't inhale anymore. It ain't gonna hurt me."

When we'd get to the gulf, we'd spend the day fishing and laughing until we ran out of things to write.

We had great friends in the Key Club, too and we could now have the show written *before* we left happy hour. People would tell us jokes and made jokes about the news to each other, and we would write their comments down. The place was very popular and had no shortage of people and humor.

We also had a lot of inspiration. The place would sell 50-cent draft beer in ten ounce frozen mugs from 4-6 P.M. That's 50-cent beers I'm telling you.

At six o'clock they would call last call for happy hour, and everyone in the place would buy 5 dollars worth. We would have 100-150 beers in front of us on the bar. Just as we were finishing those and ready to leave, they would call happy hour again from 8-9, and it was back to 50-cent beers. Geoff and I would leave no later than 9PM. We had to get to sleep to start all over again.

Geoff and I laughed for months. He was helping me chase the dream and taking my mind off of V, who I had missed but knew it was the right thing to do. Then one day after happy hour Geoff dropped a bomb. Geoff said, "Would you have a problem with me dating Veronica?"

"Wow! Geoff and Veronica… and the girls? Wow!"

What would you do if your best friend wanted to date the girl you lived with for two years? If you're me, you analyze the situation.

"I thought to myself. *"Hmm, it has been about six months. Only six months. He is a great guy. She's a great girl. They are the same age, and at a different time in my life, I wouldn't have left her. I'll always love her, well; I'll always care about her. Knowing her sure has matured me and he has been fantastic for me. I love 'em both. Hell, get together and rule the world."*

"No dude, I don't have a problem."

"It's kind of strange," He said, "I've always liked her. Even when we all worked together, even before you started dating."

"No, shit! Really? All that time?"

"Yeah,"

"Wow. Then I guess I don't have a problem."

"Life sure is weird, my friend."

"Yeah, take a shit and push me in it."

Noticing Me …They Are!

So there I was, standing on the right side of Geoff, looking at a Justice of the Peace on the beautiful grounds of a 19th century plantation, the best man at my best friend's wedding, watching him marry my ex-girlfriend. It was weird, but their family and our friends on the back lawn with the sun shining bright, dressed in various shades of linen, and smelling just a hint of magnolia, made all feel wonderful. I was happy for the two people who made me a better man. No, made me a better person. They each gave me more of the knowledge I needed to chase the dream and get noticed. V lifted my mediocre radio show to greater heights. Geoff made my writing and delivery to the point and more heartfelt, the good, the bad, and the shit that almost got me fired. It was a happy day, and love was all around us.

With the cake eaten and the bouquet thrown, the best man's mission was complete. The most surreal moment of my life was behind me, so I went to the new house I had found when the now newlywed couple weeks before told me they were getting married. I was single and once again living alone.

Trying to be convincing I kept telling myself,

"Everything is gonna be alright. You're talented. You just have to write the show on your own again that's all. You can do this." I was scared. I lost my writing partner and already missed laughing all the time.

In the cramped studio apartment the four walls of the new digs started to close in. As I agonized about my ability, the place grew smaller. I had to get out. I needed liquid reassuring so I went to the place for possible words of admiration.

When I got to the Key Club, Michelle was there, a girl I'd admired from afar for the last six months. She was tall with long legs, long dark wavy hair; she wore it up on the back of her head and had big brown eyes outlined by dark framed glasses. She was a very pretty brunette, the epitome of the hot librarian.

She seemed unattached by playing pool with the regulars, laughing and cutting up as she always did with everyone who came close. She was fun to watch.

When she bent over the pool table to make a shot I noticed she had on a tight fitting dark colored skirt. I thought that maybe she had been somewhere dressy that day, too. It reminded me that she was always well-dressed, every time with everything in place. She was also the type to always have good-looking guys around her, and I considered her way out of my league.

I was sitting next to Danny, a good friend, who noticed me staring when he said, "Why don't you wave for her to come here?" It made me think of Sal.

"Right, she'll just walk on over?"

"That's what you've got to do."

He reached out his arm and motioned for her to come to the bar. When she got there, he said, "Larry wants to buy us all a round a drinks."

She said with a big grin, "I would love one," and Danny got the free one he deserved.

"This is my friend Larry; he works at the radio station."

"It's very nice to finally meet you. I've heard so much about you," she said.

I sat up a little taller in my chair.

"You've been working at the radio station for what, about four years now?" she asked.

"Yeah, that's right"

"I've seen you in a few of the plays you've done."

"No kidding?"

"I remember when you were Grand Marshall on Mardi Gras Day. I ran up to the float, and you gave me a stuffed teddy bear. I think I still have that thing, or my son has it or something."

"You remember that?"

"Larry, I've been following your career for a while. I think you're really talented."

"I didn't think anybody was even watching."

With a big grin she said, "We should go out and do something some day."

Now, feeling ten feet tall, I half laughed, and said, "Whenever you're ready."

"Let me call a baby sitter, and we can go later."

I thought, "Wow! This day is turning out good after all."

She then turned to Danny and asked, "Would you like to go?"

"Oh, I'd love to, but I don't think my girlfriend would like that."

"Oh! That's right, you're taken, but I know Larry is safe. Let me go find a baby sitter," and she left to use the phone behind the bar.

What the hell did she mean by safe?

"Danny, what the hell was that about?"

He said with a touch of confusion, "Larry, I could be wrong here, but I think she thinks you're gay, dude."

"Jesus Christ! No wonder she wants to go out with me. She thinks I don't what to sleep with her."

Danny now has grin on his face, and I think it's funny too because now I realize what's going on.

"What are you going to do? Danny asked.

"Are you kidding me? I'm going out with her and hope she fucks her gay friend." I then shook my head and wondered how many girls do I have to sleep with to prove I'm not?

Michelle comes back from making her phone call and proceeds to tell me what she has in store for our non-date. First, she's going to pick up her son at her sister's house and bring her home. Another friend is going to baby-sit. I should just jump in with her and leave my car at the Key Club.

So off we go. It's now about 7 P.M. It's not even dark. We pick up her son at her sister's not far away and go on to her apartment. The baby-sitter is on the way, and Michelle invites me into her room to talk while she gets dressed.

She proceeds to undress in front of me, undoing her skirt, and taking off her blouse. I'm amused but why not, I'm the gay guy, right?

Stunning in a thin black bra and even skimpier see thru black panties, she proceeds to put on make-up. She's bashing her ex-husband and telling me how she loves her son, all the while innocently pushing out her ass as she leans forward over the dresser to get her face closer to the mirror. The place started to get a bit warm.

She continued with what I presumed was "girl talk" between two girlfriends, and I thought I was going to lose it when she put on red lipstick and turned to me and said, "Tell me, is this the most perfect shade of red?

Playing the part, I said in my best flamboyant gay voice, "Oh! It's *you* honey. It is definitely, you, you, you, and you."

Michelle throws on a little black dress, shakes it down, turns around, and asks me to zip her up. I do, and she turns back around and pulls the pin out of her hair. Her hair falls below her shoulders and Wow!

She then walks into her spare bedroom to wait for the sitter. That's when I felt the familiar feeling below my waist and waited. I didn't want the horse to lose just as he was coming out of the gate.

When she returned, she asked me if I wanted a Xanax. I said. "No thanks, I'm a drinker."

The knock on the door happens and we're out of there.

We jump back in her car, a sporty one at that, and while driving down the road, she said, "'Larr, I grabbed something for you to hear." As she rummaged through her purse, she said, "It took forever to find you this song. You're going to love it."

She popped in the tape, pressed the buttons on the cassette player, and out of the speakers comes the title song of "Willie Wonka and The Chocolate Factory," the slow song that Willie Wonka sings when there're all in the candy garden, something about "just another day in paradise, a world of pure imagination."

Let me remind you, I'm supposed to be the gay guy but not so gay that I won't sleep with her. I'm one of those "just needs the right kind of woman to turn me around kind of gay guy."

I said, "What a beautiful song and a movie to d-i-e, die for."

"I knew you would love it."

We stopped at a house. I wait in the car. She knocks on the door and no one answers. We do this at two other places. I figure she's trying to find something, I just don't know what it is. Actually, I don't care because I've got a pretty good buzz by now.

We end up back at the Key Club. She goes to the bathroom. Danny is still there.

"So? How's the evening going?"

"So far, she's undressed in front of me, and if she gets drunk, lonely, and wants the gay friend to cuddle, I'm going to be all over it with a completely unexpected hard-on. Danny, I'll go to my grave not knowing how it could have gotten there."

Michelle came back from the bathroom, and we had a drink. I'm drinking scotch. She's drinking white wine. After some small talk, she gets bored and says, "Let's go take a ride."

She tries the houses one more time. No one is there, and we head back to the Key Club, once more ordering drinks. This time we play a game of pool. She said she was a good pool player, so my mission now was to beat her at her own game and be cuddle worthy.

As the game progressed, she would touch my arm or hug me when she or I would make a good shot. Things were working out. I'm thinking my diabolical plan of deception just might get me laid. I won the game, and it was time to leave. We jumped in the car, and as we were driving down the road, she said, "I don't think my friends are going to be there. Why don't we just go to a strip club?"

Forgetting I'm supposed to be a gay guy I said with a happy grin, "A strip club, really?"

"You wouldn't mind, huh?"

"I guess if you want to," I said dejectedly. "I guess we can for a little while," and off we go a strip club just outside of town. I'm thinking this shit is getting good.

We walk into the "Heavenly Bodies" strip club. It was about half full of people and a strip *joint* would be a better label. The music is loud. The place is smoky, and a girl is half dressed hanging on a pole.

We both walk up to the bar, and I recognize the manager from doing a remote broadcast at another club she ran. The manager, an attractive looking woman, came over to say hello, and as she walked up to us said, "Larry, what are you doing here?"

"You know one another?" Michelle asked.

"Yeah, we go back a bit," she said and extended her hand.

I shook it lightly and said, "Yeah, We've met before."

Michele turned to speak to her, and I noticed one of Veronica's cousins and started talking to him about Geoff's wedding that afternoon. He asked me a great question. "What the hell are you doing in a strip club with someone who looks like that?"

"You don't want to know."

Talking to my friend, in between sentences, I tried to keep an eye on Michelle, who I see is floating around through the bar. After about fifteen minutes, I was concerned and went to look for her. I continued around the corner of the bar, around a partition, and there I found her with her tongue down the throat of the manager. My jaw drops. She notices me, and I apologetically hold up the palm of my hands and say, "Excuse me," and go to walk away. Michelle grabs me by the arm and says," I guess now you know. I'm gay. *Please* don't say anything. *Please* don't tell anybody."

Just then, I *really* understood what the evening was about, two *homosexuals* out on the town.

I go back to my conversation, order another scotch, a double this time and begin to laugh at the situation. Sleeping with a lesbian seems much harder than sleeping with a woman who thinks you're gay. At least a straight woman wants to have a penis inside her.

About fifteen minutes later, still talking to my friend and now the three strippers who get paid to approach patrons, I look around and see Michelle across the room. She has now jumped on the stage, grabbed the pole, and started dancing for the guys, which is now starting to piss off the strippers. After all, she looked much better than the strippers, and the guys were giving her their money.

Michelle is making a total spectacle of herself, and I'm thinking "What a night. What a night" That's when I notice a commotion. The manager comes out of the ruckus, approaches me, and says, "Larry, you better watch this bitch 'cause I'm not going to put up with her shit."

"Hey, I'm just here with her. I can't control her," I said, and I went back to my conversation.

Perhaps two minutes later, I see another commotion at the other end of the bar. The manager was yelling at Michelle pointing her finger inches from her face. Michelle said something back. I didn't know what it was. I was across the room.

Michelle shakes her head from side to side as if to say, "Go ahead bitch, hit me" and the manager rears back and punches Michelle square in the face as hard as she could.

When Michelle hit the ground, her feet went above her head. Freaked, I went to help.

When I got there, the manager pointed her finger in *my* face and said, "Get her fucking ass out of here."

I wasn't offended.

I extended my hand downward to help Michelle off her ass. She jumped up and said, "I better get the fuck out of here," and with her hand in mine, I started toward the door. When I reached the foyer, I could see in the dim light her bottom lip was cut, and she was bleeding all down her chin.

"Michelle, you're bleeding. Let me get you a napkin."

She looked at me with her eyes real wide, wiped her mouth with the back of her hand, saw the blood and licked it. Then, with a crazed look said, "Blood... I love it... I fucking love it."

That was it. It was over. I had had enough.

I thought, what the hell is this crazy ass woman about? I've got to get the hell out of here. I grab her hand and lead her to her car. We get in the car, and she realizes she left her car keys on the bar so now she wants to go back in.

I told her, "Stay your ass, where you are. I'll go back in."

The manager met me at the door holding up Michelle's keys. I got back to the car; we took off and went back to the Key Club.

Once there I got out, said good-bye, and told her she might want to go home. She said she's not usually like this, and she drove away still thinking I'm gay. I bet she went back to get some more. I didn't care. I had a full day. My best friend married my ex-girlfriend. I tried to screw a lipstick lesbian pretending I'm a gay, and now I'm safe and sound in the Key Club. I want to go home no matter how small the damn house is. I looked at the clock behind the bar and it was only 10:30. Tomorrow I had to write Monday's show. Life goes on. I went to sleep.

At work, I still saw Geoff. I would throw stuff his way and he'd give me a punch line. It was always better than mine.

Two months later I find out Geoff and V are separating. She moved out. I moved back in. For the next twelve years, Geoff and I rarely brought it up.

A Pillar of the Community

Geoff and I were back, and when asked to go to the Ice Capades in New Orleans on a school bus full of citizens from TARC, The Terrebonne Parish Association for Retarded Citizens, I figured no problem. I was flattered they would ask a lowly disc jockey at the #1 radio station in a market of one.

It was a clear Saturday morning and a bright blue sky was in store when I found out it was not one, but *three* school bus loads of TARC citizens. I hesitantly took those first steps onto the bus, and while looking down the aisle, noticing the different but same expressions all staring back, you couldn't have imagined my surprise when a representative told me that I would also be a chaperone.

These weren't kids, little rug-rats I could tower above and rule with an iron fist. They were adults; titties, balls, and all. I could barely take care of myself much less grown people, all with that weird expression, all-traipsing around the Superdome.

I sat down on an empty seat in the middle of the bus, and with a jolt that caused a noisy reaction from every one; we were on our way with me now quite leery.

As the bus pulled away from the radio station, they introduced me to the citizens I would, "keep an eye on." They were interesting to say the least.

One was a tall skinny black fellow who as soon as the bus started rolling kept laughing while throwing himself back into his seat. He was laughing at nothing in particular. He just kept laughing and laughing throwing himself back and forth with his mouth open wide and gleaming smile. Oddly enough, as we rode to our destination some sixty miles away, he would stand up, with an arm out the little window and yelled at people outside the bus. He'd scream at women, "Hey baby! You fine! We're coming back to pick you up later!" They'd wave back, and he'd laugh some more.

He saw city workers in orange vests leaning on their shovels and yelled, "Get to work! We pay your money!" One guy flipped him the finger. He started laughing hysterically. The son-of-a gun laughed for six straight hours. I still laugh thinking about it.

There was another guy who called himself the "King of TARC."

"I'm bigger than Elvis," he said. "I'm the king. Don't mess with me. You want something done, you ask me."

Unaware of his realm, I said, "You do know the king is dead, don't you?"

He looked at me with contempt and slowly raised his chin and said, "I said don't mess with me." I didn't.

I noticed the king could get the other citizens to listen to him so he had some panache. I figured he was the alpha male. He also had girlfriends.

One was very meek and mousy, but when his attention was on something else and couldn't hear, she whispered to me, "Don't listen to him. He be so stupid. He always thinks he something."

Her name was Paula, and I was surprised when she told me how much she loves her job.

"You know, I got a job?"

"You do, huh?"

"Want to see my paycheck?"

"Sure."

She dug into her purse and held up a check for $12.52.

"I'm a worker at the Country Store. I make over twelve dollars a week."

"Really? That's so cool."

The Country Store sold arts and crafts that the citizen's hand made on the campus of TARC. She also cleaned tables at the restaurant, which I found out was located next to the country store.

Proudly and with a bit of in your face sarcasm, she said, "See? I got a job." The gleam in her eyes conveying that it wasn't just twelve dollars and fifty-two cents; she was a citizen of the *entire* community not just of the TARC community. It was my first lesson of the day.

There was also a younger girl who looked about eighteen years old. Janey seemed distant. She was dressed more artistically than the others with a flowery shirt and jeans that had colorful patches placed strategically all around her pants, her distraught denim looking retro. She stared comfortably out the window, and I quietly asked a counselor about her. The counselor told me the girl rarely talks and showed me a small ceramic clown-pin attached to her blouse.

"She hand-made this," the counselor said, pointing to her own shoulder.

Nodding, I said, "It's beautiful," and it was.

The girl over heard and smiled at me briefly but then went back to what had her attention outside in the distance.

"She sells more things at the store than anyone else," the counselor said. I was impressed and another lesson learned.

I leaned over the counselor and said to Janey, "You're very talented. You have a wonderful gift for making things."

She smiled brightly, and I felt I was in the right place at the right time.

There was a lull in the adventure, the bus rolling along, swaying with the road, I was being amused at all the different people who somehow looked alike when I noticed a rather pear shaped fellow starring at me, head tilted slightly downward, mouth open, with a very odd look. He seemed about thirty-five, narrow shouldered, and round at the hips. His hair was cut short and it made his ears look big. After a minute or so he said, "Hey!" I looked toward him and asked, "Yeah man, what's up?"

"This girls my heaven!" and he pointed to the round girl sitting next to him. She smiled very coy, and he went abruptly back to the blank expression and the opened mouth stare. My thought, "That was weird."

He awakes, and while pointing to her, says, "Hey! Without her I don't know what I'd do. She's my heaven."

Smiling I said, "That's cool, man. You're a lucky guy."

Embarrassed, she smiled again, and he once more went to the opened mouth stare.

He comes back to us again, a moment later, and says, "Hey! You look like my cousin."

"No kidding? Your cousin has red hair?"

"No."

"Does your cousin have a red beard?" (I had grown one.)

"Hell no, he ain't got red hair. He ain't got a red beard... I ain't seen him in ten years. I don't know what he looks likes."

I thought I was going to die. This guy was telling me I look like the cousin he hasn't seen in ten years, and his cousin doesn't look anything like me.

That's when I really started to have fun. I started to go from seat to seat and talk with all of the citizens on the bus. This shit was on.

I would yell to the whole group, "Does everybody have their skates?" and they all looked at me wide-eyed.

"When we get to the place, we have to practice our turns!" I was working the room. "Does everybody know how to skate?"

The things they would say were so interesting, and then all of a sudden they would say something totally off the wall and completely understand why they are on the bus.

When we got to the Dome, the powers that be must have misinterpreted my enthusiasm as being responsible and added a few more citizens for me to "keep an eye on." It didn't matter because I now understood my role, that of a brother, a friend, and a person who got roped into this scenario that TARC created. I was also told to really keep an eye on this one little fellow and his girlfriend.

They both looked about thirty years old, five feet tall, each were two hundred pounds, and had Down Syndrome. I noticed them on the bus holding hands and could see they relied on one another for comfort. It was quite cute.

To these two citizens the Dome seemed massive and walking down the steps to the rink, the girl was latched on to me. The stairs frightened her. She was sticking her fingernails in my arm. She wasn't frantic, just focused on getting down safely with a death grip. I was her support. I was glad I could help.

Her buddy was hanging on my other side but not nearly as tight, more so locked arm in arm. It took what seemed like hours to get to the floor since they took very small steps, and we were walking down those stairs that are just over one stride apart so they each struggled to take two footsteps for each step.

We got down to the rink, and our seats were two rows from the ice. I thought, "Damn, I've never seen ice skating like this before. This is great." The ice looked so smooth, and the skaters practicing made the sound of the blades on the ice poetic. Each stride was long and beautiful but as soon as we sat down, my two new friends who had brought money said they wanted something from the concession stand. I decided if we get something we should get it before the show and with the line being extremely long, as slowly as you can imagine, we walked back up the long flight of two step stairs to the concession stand.

Now before we left the bus the counselor did tell me to watch the little guy because he does like to eat. I said I would, assuming I'd just wipe his chin if he got a little too rambunctious with a burger.

So, we're now in the concession line. I'm doing alright, talking and learning with each sentence my "buds" throw out at me. As I looked around the Dome, I noticed Jay from the old neighborhood in New Orleans. I told my two new friends, "Look. I'm going to be right over there." It was about sixty feet, thirty yards.

"I can see everything you do, Okay. I'm not going to leave you. I'll be right over there. Do you see where I'll be?" They nodded yes. "Good."

My friend and I were talking, and I could see the citizen's move up a few feet. I would talk more while facing them and kept a close watch. I could see they were okay and I'd talk more and kept looking. They were now close to the concession stand. I talked more, and they were making their order at the counter. I could see them clearly, and they were getting along very well. Everything was fine.

I looked again.

"Holy Shit!"

The two of them were slowly on their way back. She had three powder-candy straws that looked four feet long and as round as a roll of paper towels. She looked like a cokehead with powder all around her mouth, and my new buddy had two armloads full of junk food.

The little fellow returned with two hot dogs, a plate of nachos, a large drink, a snowball, and an ice cream cone. His arms were loaded as if he was going to the last supper. Plus, I knew the ice cream would start melting.

I quickly said good-bye to my friend and ran to get some napkins. I wiped the little guy's arms and took the two hot dogs and the snowball. I then talked him out of the drink. He wasn't giving up the ice cream and nachos for anything.

We started to our seats, ever so slowly, both taking three-inch steps. I could feel the entire Dome watching me as we went all the way down the stairs to the second row. When we sat down, I thought everything was going to be okay. That's when he looked at me with the funniest face, a face that to this day, still amuses me. His eyes were wide open, and he looked so confused but in my newfound wisdom I read his mind.

Smiling, looking at the cutest little man in the world I said, "You having trouble there, buddy?" Still wide eyed, he nodded slowly, yes.

"Buddy, I'll tell you what. Why don't you eat the ice cream, and I'll hang on to the snowball. I'm going to put the drink right here on the floor. We'll get to those hot dogs soon as we can, and if you can swallow anything else, the nachos are going to be right next to the drink. Would you like that?"

He was convinced.

By intermission the food was gone and he, I would think, completely full, and sick to his stomach. Thank goodness I didn't get in any trouble, and I actually enjoyed the ice capades.

We got back to the bus, and the counselor had heard about the food incident. She just laughed and said, "Don't worry about it. He probably had the time of his life watching all the action with all that food."

"He might be sick when he gets home," I said.

"Aw, don't worry about it. There's not much we can do and it won't be the first time."

...

It was much more subdued on the bus ride home. Most were tired, but the skinny guy was still laughing, Elvis was still the king, and I had started to get my fill of being a chaperone for the citizens of TARC.

As I got up to leave, standing in the row of people to exit the bus I was stopped next to the counselor sitting by the girl who made the pretty pin. The counselor turned, motioned me down to her level, and said softly, "Janey wants to give you this pin." Putting up my palms I said, "I can't take that."

The young girl looked at me, squinted, then looked back at the counselor, and adamantly shook her head yes as if to say, "Make him do it." The counselor then unpinned the charm from her blouse and handed it to me, then said, "This is a thank you. Thanks for coming to help."

"I can't accept this," I told her. "I should be giving something to them."

"No, Larry, she wants to do it. Really, you've given plenty, more than you know."

Janey looked up at me from her seat and said two syllables while moving her head up and down deliberately. The words came out "Tank coo," but I knew what she meant. Oh, my God, I knew exactly what she meant. The hair stood up on my arms. My eyes started to water, and I said. "No, Janey. Thank *you*. I thank you."

I'll never forget that day. I learned a lot about the TARC community, and now know so much more about their world, how they intermingle, act and react, love and are loved, by one another and the people around them. Damn, their world is just like ours. I learned that day, their world *is* ours.

Remarkably these days some of the citizens still recognize me and say I'm their "Radio Buddy." I did run into "Elvis" years later.

"Yo, man! You're the King of TARC. What's up?"

"Don't you say that. I ain't Elvis."

"No, don't you remember? You were the King of TARC. We were on the bus together. Remember?"

"Don't you say that kind of stuff."

"Oh, wow, I'm sorry. I'm really sorry, dude," and he walked away. I do see him every now and then, when I talk to him I don't bring it up.

And, the fellow who thought I looked like his cousin lives in my neighborhood. He catches the TARC bus two corners down. The bus isn't yellow anymore. It's painted red, white and blue and has "Patriots" written on the side, an appropriate mascot. I wave to him when I stop at the stop sign.

Pulling away I wonder what his cousin now looks like.

Wait Till You See The Tub

In time Geoff would leave the radio station disillusioned by the people who would suck up his talent, something many with the dream succumb to. He would get his real estate license and try that. It's one of the many things he would do, but just like before we got up very early each weekday to write my radio show.

Many talented and creative people do give up. They have children or get married so their family demands it. Or, something happens beyond their control, having to be a caretaker, unforeseen consequences, or they're going to put it on the back burner and accidently turn off the stove, not to mention age. Time waits for no one.

One particular morning Geoff was at the typewriter when he looked in the corner of the room and asked, "Larry, what did you do with your shotguns?" I looked in the corner and saw the empty gun rack. We both looked at each other and instantly got up to check the other parts of the house. Gone were the guns, my hunting stuff, the microwave, the stereo, and some things out of his room. We sat back down, decided to call the cops, and while waiting, Geoff said, "You know we really should get out this neighborhood. If you want to go in with me, I've got the perfect house, a house with a pool inside."

"You mean an indoor pool?"

"No. I mean a pool inside the house."

"What do you mean a pool inside the house?"

"A freaking pool, inside the house. I'll show it you, Guido."

Geoff had it listed, and I was in before I saw it.

This was one badass pad. It was an octagon shaped house made of cedar and cherry wood. It looked round from the street, and when you walked in, you noticed it didn't have any walls. It was just a big octagon shaped room with a high octagon shaped ceiling that had exposed rafters that rose upward to a sky light in the middle. All around the house was indirect lighting that shined toward the roof. The shadows created against those rafters were magnificent. It looked like a ski lodge with a red cone shaped fireplace. The floor was rust colored cement with broken inlayed rock but the best thing about it was a completely indoor heated pool in a connected room to the back. It was actually the pool area that my bed was going in.

If you walked straight as you entered a decorative wrought iron front door, you walked across the house, then down the steps of the shallow end of a pool. It was bad-ass.

Each morning I would get out of my waterbed, which V let me have, walk four steps and jump into a heated indoor pool.

While swimming you could see the rest of the house and with the stone floors you could get out of the pool and walk into the kitchen. The house was designed in a way that it had an open bathroom around a partition and a small area with a toilet that was closed in, it just big enough to fit. Geoff said, "That should keep the big eaters out."

"But Geoff, big eaters are the ones that use the bathroom the most."

"They can't eat in there. Besides, that would be redundant."

The bathroom area had a sunken black tub with gold fixtures completely surrounded by mirrors. A local architect built this thing in-between wives, and it looked like it came out of a seventies Playboy Magazine.

Geoff and I went in half; total cost an eye-popping and very inexpensive $19,000. I signed my name for $9,500, but living with a pool in my bedroom was priceless.

Through the years, living in the home, I would leave then Geoff would live there and cover the note. Then, I would come back and Geoff would leave. Or maybe we were both unattached and living together again.

In all the years together Geoff said only one negative thing to me. "Please don't put knives in the soapy water in the sink. My mother cut her hand, I don't want to cut mine." Other than that we were best friends, perfect roommates, and a soul mate I didn't have to ruin by sleeping with. We were together chasing the dream, writing the show. and living in one cool-ass pad.

We would have parties after the Key Club would close. People would come over and see the pool in the bedroom and say you must have a lot of sex in the pool. I'd say, "Not really. Come see the tub." With the mirrors reflecting back and forth you'd see ass for days, an orgy of two. It was "cribs" before MTV had "Cribs." I was still just a small time announcer leaving Houma tomorrow but now had one of the baddest bachelor pads in town and at a starving artist price. Our note was $180.00 a month. My rent was $90.00. Good God almighty.

It was now 1987, and for the next four years, Geoff and I wrote plays, wrote dating games, standup comedy, and MC'd shows for different acts in clubs and for benefits throughout the area. He wrote comedy for me and other comedians in town. One of the comedians was a Justice of the Peace. Geoff wrote him jokes, and the guy married him and Geoff's third wife for free. Plus, during that time I found out the radio station was moving to New Orleans. Finally, I was going back home. Get good at my craft and the chance at the New Orleans market was coming. What luck, I was chasing the dream, and it was going to come to me. I knew when I got to New Orleans I'd start doing theater at night and play radio during the day. That was my plan. Then one night in walked a guy who would become another great friend. He believed in me and had plans for me, too.

...

I was at the Key Club hanging out, mentally writing the show, and enjoying the people. I made some very good friends there. The owner and the bartenders would attend the plays and I was even allowed to cash a check. Many people weren't, and it flattered me. It was never more than twenty bucks since I was buying fifty-cent beers, for Christ's sake.

Danny said, "You're always here during happy hour, Hyatt." Both of our eyes got big and the name stuck. They even threw me a birthday party and bought me a baseball cap that said, "Happy Hour Hyatt" and a shirt that they had airbrushed that read, "Don't mind the glare from my red hair, it's just big Larr."

I got the "Big Larr" nickname from something Geoff would do when he was bored. If I was talking to a woman for a while, he could see we were hitting it off. He would then seize that opportunity and walk into our conversation. Remember, Geoff is a character.

"Oh, so you know my roommate Larry? He's a great guy, isn't he"?

The girl would have to say yes or nod her head, and Geoff would pipe up with, "From what I hear he has a really big penis, too."

I would roll my eyes with embarrassment while they would roll theirs. Then pretend shock as I tell Geoff to go away.

"Don't mind my friend. Look, I don't have a neck, but I got a big dick. It's a curse I know, but it's something I have to live with, "God giveith and god takeith away."

It didn't get women to jump into bed with me, but it did work in the long run. No pun intended. Well, yeah, I went with a dick joke. What I'm saying is the the Key Club was very blue-collar.

I was sitting at the bar shooting the shit when in walked a guy wearing a baseball uniform, one of the older nylon tight fitting kind. He came in with three extremely attractive women. He was slim, with light hair, 5' 10", and a good-looking guy. It appeared that they had just come off the playing field and were there to celebrate a win.

As they played pool, he had a way about him that showed confidence. Not a swagger but a noticeable charisma, shaking hands with everyone who came close. There was something about this guy that just made him cool. He had that something I would have called, "it." One of the girls had bought the drinks and brought them back to him. I thought that was really smooth. Sometime later he came over to the bar to get a drink.

"Excuse me... Larry? Right?"

"Yeah, how do you do?"

"Good... I'm good. My name's Lenny," and we shook hands.

"I've seen you in some of those plays you do."

"Really? No kidding?"

"Yeah, my girlfriend makes me go."

I let out a laugh. "Well thanks, and you in a baseball suit, what? You just got off the stage from staring in, Damn Yankees?"

"Okay, Okay, I'll give you that one."

I took a double take.

"You've heard of Damn Yankees?"

"No. But I'm smart enough to know you were giving me back a shot."

We smiled at one another and nodded in agreement.

Lenny told me he was putting together a nightclub with "a lot of things going on." He envisioned bartenders jumping on the bar and dancing, bartenders blowing fire and flipping bottles when they make the drinks. He was looking for a disc jockey that could create some excitement. He said he'd like me to see what I thought of the idea and that he had it all written down in a book, the whole plan, what he wanted to call it, what he wanted to happen there, and how it would incorporate all the employees in the club. I was intrigued. He took my number, and that was it. He said he'd keep in touch and went back to the group. A couple of days later he called at the radio station and asked if we could meet.

We met back at "The Club," and he had his notebook. He ordered a couple of beers and then suggested we go somewhere quiet to explain everything.

He seemed relaxed but excited about his project, and I found out he was from Buffalo, New York, and came down here for the oil field business years ago. His uncle came first and told him about it. He did well and was supposed to go back but really liked it here and stayed because he liked the people. Well, that certainly sounded familiar.

He was my age so we had plenty to talk about. He was smart, up on current events, and knew politics, all things I enjoy. He was gracious and after awhile we decided to go to his apartment and discuss the venture. At his place, a very nicely furnished loft style apartment, we discussed the endeavor.

He offered me a seat, and as he sat on the sofa said, "Here's my idea," and pulled out the notebook, placed it on the glass coffee table, and proceeded to tell me of the club.

On the first page of the notebook was the name of the club in big print, "Illusions," and he spoke of a place where if you were on a first date or by yourself there would be things to see and things to talk about so you wouldn't get bored. First date couples would be entertained, single guys could talk to girls about what's happening around them, and everybody else would be there because it's the hottest place in town. It sounded logical to me. All of this was written down in the book.

He wanted magicians in the place to go along with the name Illusions. They would do their act on stage or go from table to table and do slight of hand. The owners would wear white tuxedo jackets and greet patrons at the door.

He had a barber chair that people would sit in, and the big buxom blond would kick you back and pour shots directly into your mouth, throw you back up real fast then spin you around.

The décor would be very woman friendly with Negals on the walls, plenty of mirrors to give it more illusions, an elaborate fountain, and a wooden dance floor that shined. All this was in the book; all of this was in the plan.

The next thing caught me completely off guard.

Maybe he was smart enough to go for my ego, I don't know, but as he read I followed.

"This is where Larry Hyatt comes in. He will control the stage and everything on it. When Larry plays a Stevie Wonder, song he'll put on the beaded wig and sunglasses and imitate Stevie. When Larry plays the song "Strokin," he will get people on stage and do the strokin dance. If Larry says we do something on stage, we do it. Larry will teach the bartenders to dance on the bars or in back of the bars or where ever they can. Whatever Larry thinks the club should do to entertain, Larry will show us, and we'll learn it."

Now let's get back to ego. I've got one, but it's in check. Believe me, I knew I was just a piss-ant DJ in a very small market getting very little money and trying to get back to New Orleans. I'm twenty-eight, my love is theater, and this guy wants to give me a stage. But why the hell is my name already in the book? This guy is just telling me about it for the first time. What if I wasn't interested? What if I thought it would never work? He would certainly have to tear out some of the pages.

"Lenny, umm, I'm amazed you have my name written down there. You didn't even know what I thought of the idea."

"Larry, you are the only one in this town who can do this. You have everything I'm looking for. I can't do it without you."

This guy was good.

"Lenny," I said, "I love the idea. It sounds like it would work. But you're calling the place Illusions. I can impersonate all these people and make it illusions of the character. I'll white my hair and be Frank Sinatra. I'll put on the costumes and be Elton John. I'm sure I could get people together and rehearse the acts."

We started spouting off bands we could impersonate: Kiss, B-52s, Joe Cocker, Hank Williams Jr., popular fifties and sixties groups, it was endless.

I said, "Dude, I'll make it a Vegas type show with full costumes. I know a little about making costumes. Just get somebody to play the records until I get all that make-up off."

"No problem."

"Damn this is cool. It's so original," I said.

"Yeah, no one has ever done this."

"Oh, it's been done. I think they called it vaudeville."

We called it vaudeville of the 80's, and I was hooked. I asked, "When can we get started?"

"I have to come up with a little more money and find the right place that meets the criteria. There is something else. You must be able to see the stage from everywhere in the building."

This some-bitch is real good.

We shook hands, and I said I'm in. I told him I was leaving Houma to go back to New Orleans, but when the station leaves town, I'll come back and open the place. I now was looking forward to my own "nightclub act." Eight years of radio was enough. I'm going to get ready for the theatre. I'll start getting ideas and working them in my head and putting things down on paper. I'm finally getting a stage of my own.

In life things take time. For twelve long months I would be getting ready for my stage show. I would see Lenny out on the town, and each time he would tell me "it's almost there." He would once again, excitingly, and with the same passion, tell me about this club he was going to start, and I would tell him. "I'm in." again and again, and again. To be honest I was doing radio and chasing the dream, I would be moving home shortly, so I didn't long for an outlet like the time I quit school.

My life was going well. I continued to be in all the plays and musicals: Seymour in, "Little shop of Horrors," Billis in "South Pacific," Sky in, "Guys and Dolls," I won a couple of awards for best actor and supporting actor at the Le Petit Theatre banquets. I was judging beauty pageants and making television appearances, the master of ceremonies, plus, I kept hearing the station was moving to New Orleans. I was ready to get back home. I stayed entirely too long in this very small market.

My fears were confirmed when the station manager said to me that I didn't have nine years of radio experience; I had three years of experience three times. How could I have been so stupid?

I was wasting my time, but hey, I was going back to New Orleans any day now, right? The rollercoaster is still moving to the top. Then the shock of the business hit me dead in the face.

"You will be rewarded," I was told for three long years. "The station is moving to New Orleans. We'll have a place for you, on or off the air." But that wasn't the case. The station was sold, and I'm not going anywhere. The homecoming for all the people who believed in me before I left, a very long nine years ago, is now a wash. They bent me over. They could have at least kissed me first. I wasted those years. I stayed a long time for this company, living only on chasing the dream.

I spoke to Geoff that night. He had quit real estate and started going to school to be a boat captain in Galveston. He started in the galley and now was a captain on the bridge. He started as a dishwasher; each time returning home, he would take another test and get promoted. He was not only funny but also bright.

"Larry, let's move to Texas," he said. "We'll rent the house and get the hell out of here. Let me show you Galveston. I love the place. It's like nothing I ever seen before. You can audition for some shows and test the waters. Maybe get something in Houston. We'll write when I'm in, and you can get your standup comedy chops. You're good, Guido. You can do it. You had a good run."

"Yeah, I guess it's time."

I called Lenny that night to tell him what happened. He said, "Larry, I was just going to call you. Today we signed the papers for a building that is perfect."

"You're kidding me?"

"I've got the keys in my pocket."

The thought of having my own stage close to my $90 a month home was much more persuasive than packing up and moving to a new town.

"Lenny, Geoff and I are going to take a vacation to Texas."

"Don't stay, Larry. We are ready to set up your stage."

"I'm going but I'm coming back," and when I hung up the phone, I realized I haven't taken a vacation that didn't put me in New Orleans in nine years. I could never afford one.

Geoff and I returned from Galveston, but on the air that Monday, I was going through the motions. I went back on Tuesday and told the program director I was quitting in two weeks.

"Larry, you've been here a lot longer than I have. I don't need a two week notice. You've proven yourself many times over."

"Then, I'm out of here and thanks."

We shook hands and radio was over.

As I packed up my nine years worth of memories, it all kept coming back. Each item I put into that box brought back another moment, a scene, another reach, another grasp at the dream.

I had an actual bottle of "Funky Cold Medina," which was really a bottle of grape juice that came in the mail along with the record. I thought, "Damn, they're sending liquor along with the music now. I can't wait to get a song from Guns and Roses; maybe they'll send the good shit."

I saw a picture of the radio station staff from years ago with Katie standing on one end smiling and me on the other, taken before we had the "date." I stared at it, touched its frame, and on my tongue could taste a faint twelve-year-old scotch.

I found a picture of V and me with pie on my face. I had a bet with her on the Swap Shop that I would win a race we had on top of Ringling Brothers and Barnum and Bailey Circus elephants. I lost the heat but didn't lose the race because into my life she came and into it brought what she didn't know she would: knowledge, a sense of family, and a bigger swagger for turning the Swap Shop into a young career milestone.

I also found the program and a picture of the "Chicago Knockers," a group of strippers I mud wrestled as a promotion as the morning show host of All Hits KCIL. They told me to have fun and, "Let's just throw each around and make a good show of it." I listened. She lied. They whipped my ass. It was on TV for the entire town to see, and it was extremely embarrassing. I won't go into it. Find the tape.

I found the promotional picture of me with five Playboy playmates I had interviewed before I took them on a limousine ride to dinner and then to a show they did in a local nightclub called "Fantasies." Boy, you could say that again.

When I interviewed them that morning on the radio, I was shocked to see they looked like any girl off the street, seriously.

When they walked down the stairs of the hotel and to the limousine, they were absolutely stunning. When I looked at them across the table at dinner, I understood why they call them Playmates and why millions of men around the world look at them with lurid eyes.

I remembered the wine, the women, and the songs, especially when I took down from the wall the platinum record of "Joan Jett and the Black Hearts" and placed it in that box. It was to be my first record on the wall. It reminded me of all the songs that touched people's lives and became songs of the 80's.

Imagine me, one of the first people to rip open the paper envelop that it was mailed in, place it on a turntable, and hear for the first time music that I loved so much as child, the songs that this time, the entire world would sing together.

And finally when I reached some old letters from the swap shop, my first show, the ones that flattered and kept, I felt an accomplishment pass over me, and it was time for a new adventure.

To this day I hear some of those old songs that I played on the radio, close my eyes and transport myself back to "Family Tradition" and the first night I got into radio was pulled on a dance floor and thought what a town, what a town.

I picked up the box containing my career, put it on my shoulder, headed out and said the last goodbyes. I was used and discarded. I didn't want to leave this way. I got in the car and not knowing quite what to do, drove around for hours with the tears streaming down my face. I owned a very small Dodge Colt by then and only got wet if I opened the sunroof. I was crying like a blubbering baby. I started to embarrass myself when I hyperventilated.

I cried it out and went to the new building which would be my new home. Workers were inside painting the walls and ripping out the DJ booth from the middle of the stage. Lenny had said, "Larry needed that space for the show, and they better get after it." I grabbed a paintbrush and started painting.

Underneath a table, cramped, bent down on the floor, painting a baseboard, it struck me as weird. I had a new plan, and I was scared. I'm still chasing, but what the hell am I searching for?

From that stage came a view I had never expected. A show people still remind me of when they reminisce of the fun inside. That notebook was right. Houma had never seen anything like this.

Star of Stage, Screen and Magazine

The view from that stage was the most beautiful thing I'd ever seen and when the building was filled to capacity, it took my breath away. Never before had I experienced thunderous applause. Never before had people yelled my name.

Larry! Larry! Larry! Larry! It was overwhelming.

Every variety show, every voice lesson, every guitar lesson, piano lesson, stupid little kid show I did in the backyard now seemed worth it. It now had meaning. I finally knew what I was, and it scared the living shit out of me. How the hell am I to entertain a city, the lowly DJ, me, the buffoon?

George, who I knew at the radio station, was managing the place. He also wore the white tuxedo coat along with Lenny and his business partner which made our management look more dashing, outshining anything other clubs were doing. George would become a great friend and producer, and for weeks we painted, corked, cleaned, chipped, hammered and would polyurethane this building to make it the most beautiful club the town had ever seen.

Also, on the first day when I had that paintbrush in my hand, I would meet Jesse, "The J-Man" a guy who would become my right hand man. George would work the music when I was getting dressed for the next show. J-Man was a bartender, who when I needed a second person, would leave the bar and join the show. That was Lenny's idea, to use people who were employed so they would be there. I would do the acts by myself, but if I needed another Blues Brother, I grabbed J-Man. If I did a comedy bit, I grabbed J-Man.. If I needed one other person for anything, J-Man was the go to guy.

A dressing room was built, and I was in my glory. It had long shelves of wigs and racks of costumes for all the different entertainers we would do "Illusions" of, a make-up mirror with lights, and a sink but stopped short of a shower. I figured there would be entirely too much drunken-ass-naked going on after closing with a shower. I knew what I was there to do, entertain, and didn't what to lose sight of the mission.

Then I surrounded myself with actors and actresses, dancers and comedians. I called everyone I worked with to put on a show, the show, my show.

I met with a few who I worked with from the theatre department at Nicholls State, the local college. Most snubbed me. They were the elite theater people who didn't think my stupid little barroom act was anything they wanted to get involved in. I was second rate until they realized performing is learning and not every theatre dream happens when you reach twenty-two years old and graduate from college with a (say it through your teeth) theatre degree.

When those asshole students did speak to me and realized that at least I had a gig, they asked to join. You know what I told them? I told "them," the elite "theatre people."

"I would be honored to have you join us. I can certainly use someone with your talent."

I didn't say to them that humility is a bitch. They got it. Young people don't realize that many before them had the dream and that many before them were going to set the world on fire just like they are.

I ended up doing over one hundred and fifty acts. It was now vaudeville of the ninety's, and it could still work today, theater in a bar, something to look at while you got drunk. We weren't at the mouth of the river, but entertaining is universal. It's so simple.

We got pretty drunk too, and I learned fast to be careful with free liquor so close to a stage.

The first week we were open, about the fifth day, Jesse and I were on stage for the Blues Brothers. The lights were down, and we were back-to-back with our arms folded in the dark waiting for the music to begin. The place could see our silhouettes so they started to yell in anticipation of the show. Over my shoulder, I said to Jesse, "Dude, I don't think I'll be able to do the cartwheel at the beginning."

"You got a buzz, huh?"

"I sure do, and that's bullshit. These people are here to see a show."

"You're right; they deserve better…Buy you drink when we get off this thing?"

"Ya damn straight, my bro."

We still drank after that, but it wasn't enough to stop me from doing a cartwheel.

The "Illusions Players" were a rag tag team of actors who got paid with free drinks, and the lines to see us were unbelievably long. On weekends they went around the entire building. I shit you not, the entire building. The times were kick ass, and the money kept rolling in. I saw what could be made, and I wished I had owned the place, but my place was on stage. That's what I do. That's why people like me.

One of the more memorable numbers was James Brown. I blacked my skin and did a full costume impersonation, gold cape, tight pants, big hair and the moves. I got one on the police officers to hand cuff me and bring me around the back of the building, past the long line and through the front door. People thought a customer was getting arrested.

When I got to the stage, the cop took the handcuffs off, and George said into the microphone over the crowd, "On loan from the Louisiana State Penitentiary, for one night only, the one and only, the God Father of soul, the hardest working man in show business, ladies and gentlemen, put your hands together for…Mr. James Brown." The music would down beat, and I would sing it. "I Feel Good... Na na na na na …. I knew that I would now."

The place went wild.

Being an impersonator worked for me personally because I had red hair. Ninety percent of the artists I became had a different shade of hair color. When I was someone else, I never looked much like "me" so when I was on stage my look was changed from my regular appearance. Plus, the stage was high above the dance floor and much lower than the upper balcony so the audience couldn't make out my height. It was never a factor.

Blacking my skin today would probably get me shot. But I'm white. If I wanted to look like the black artists I impersonated, I had to use make-up. No one told me it was politically incorrect because it wasn't a joke. I really became those artists.

I did some cool and crazy stuff on that stage, but I would get to the dressing room after a great new number, bathe in the glory for only about fifteen minutes, and then try to figure out what the hell was I to do next, to entertain. Once again, it played on my mind. I had to keep updating the show. It wasn't easy.

The people who came every night would see a performance over and over again. I had to keep thinking of new bits. In the words of Henny Youngman, "I don't need a new act. I needed a new audience."

We impersonated Jerry Lee Lewis and lit a piano on fire. Actually, I impersonated Dennis Quaid from the movie Great Balls of Fire. There was Kenny and Dolly, Sonny and Cher, Bob Seeger, Michael McDonald, Joe Cocker, Pee

Wee Herman, Hank Williams Jr., The B-52's, Meatloaf, The California Raisin's, (Mother Mary made the costumes), black men such as Stevie Wonder, Clarence Carter, or Sir Mix A Lot where we danced to "Baby Got Back." We stuffed our pants with enormously big butts and just danced on stage. I would white my hair and sing Frank Sinatra, black my body and sing Aaron Neville. It was all straight up. I wasn't making fun of anyone. I wanted to be dead on. I was an actor who wanted to stretch my limits and, I was good at it. Or at least that's what they told me. I also made shit up. It was theatre in a bar, vaudeville.

People loved a number called the "Silhouettes on the Shade." During the song "Silhouettes on the Shade," my friend Paige and I put on body suits, put street clothes over them and acted out the song behind a screen to create a silhouette.

During the performance we'd strip off our clothes as we acted out the song in the silhouette.

On a whim I said, "Paige, turn around." She turned around and with her back to me she bent over from the waist and I started humping.

What a silhouette that was.

To this day people thought it was the funniest number they ever saw. It worked because the song was innocent, but the silhouette was risqué and not the performance. It got us in deep shit with the local officials. It wasn't long before Prince created his silhouette controversy at Super Bowl XL!

Opening night, after weeks of sweating blood to get this vision ready, George and I were the last ones to leave. The hundreds of people were now gone, and the place looked like it had one hell of a party. Confetti was on the floor, and the place looked trashed. For weeks while working, Lenny told George and me about the women we were going to meet.

"There will be women everywhere," he said. "You two will have your pick," but there was George and I, alone, together, two hard legs, in the club with confetti on the floor and the smell of stale whiskey in the room.

Thinking about the night, George said, "Larry, I've known you for a long time."

"Yeah, we do go back, huh?"

"I've seen you do a bunch of different stuff on stage, but I gotta to tell you this, when we started the show tonight, I dimmed the lights in the club, and started the music to "New York, New York," and with that big band sound, and you as Frank, under that blue light, the cigarette smoke rising above your head, I got chills."

"Yeah well, I always liked the 40's era."

"But then you turned around and you looked just like Frank Sinatra, you became the shit. This town is in for a ride."

It was one of the nicest things anybody had ever said to me. I had my own stage and my peers noticed.

One week I couldn't come up with anything new and took my furniture from my house and put it on stage. My whole living room was moved to the stage, even the clock on the wall and the telephone. It was stupid, but it worked.

It was performance art. All the while the nightclub was kicking, and people joined me on stage. We ordered pizza and had the Domino's man come up on stage and bring us the pizza. (Oh, he stayed and drank for free, the whole time saying he was going to get fired.) We got actors to pretend they were cops and came in to tell us to turn down the music because the neighbors were complaining, a jab at the residents who complained of the traffic that constantly went through their neighborhood.

We would have to announce at 2 A.M. "Please, ladies and gentleman do not go down Prevost Street. Please go to the highway to exit the property. Ladies and gentleman please do not go down Prevost Street."

I found Lenny in the crowd and asked if I could hire a choreographer during the day. I thought, let's throw some dancing girls into the mix and go "Viva Las Vegas" Lenny said, "No problem, anything for the show."

It was that night when people were just jumping on stage, that a female acquaintance had a guy along that I thought I recognized. We kept glancing at one another, each of us not wanting to say anything.

Finally he came to me and asked if I was from New Orleans. That confirmed my suspicion. It was Walter, a guy who grew up in my old neighborhood.

It was always good to see old friends in Houma because with Houma located off the beaten path, transplants didn't run into old friends unless their friends had a good reason to be in the city. Walter was now a helicopter pilot and was working at the Houma airbase for a couple of weeks.

Over the noise of the crowd he asked about my sister Kellie. Then my brother came into question. We were both assured everyone was fine, talking old times and reminiscing. When I mentioned Thomas Jefferson Middle School, he started talking about Sherwood Forest Elementary.

Over the music he said, "Hey Larry, you sang a lot in kindergarten. I'm not surprised you're doing this kind of thing."

"Holy Shit! Don't even mention Sherwood Forest. I cried when I started that school."

He laughed and said, "Man, you were hysterical. You cried so much I remember what you wore."

Completely shocked I said, "Are you kidding me? You remember what I wore on my first day of school?

Still very much amused he said, "Larry, you were wearing a white shirt, white pants, red suspenders and a little red bow tie."

Never Give Up...For No One

Lenny got a choreographer, and each day rehearsing with very agile leotard dressed female dancers then performing in the hottest club at night, packed to the hilt, is something all straight men with twinkle-toes should do, at least once.

With the new addition "The Illusion's Players" started doing elaborate dances from music videos, the ghouls from Thriller, Rhythm Nation, and the finale from Dirty Dancing, which had everyone putting down their drinks to dance along with us.

For Halloween we did Rocky Horror Picture Show, Monster Mash, and Werewolves of London and then started to do themes for the different holidays.

We did a live telethon on HTV, the local television station, and raised money for the soldiers of Desert Storm. We did the latest fads such as Velcro Jumping, Hawaiian

Tropic Beauty Contests and Dwarf Catapult; we were the shit. I wanted to get gators to retrieve the dwarfs and bring them back to the catapult, but Lenny didn't want to mess with Department of Health. "We're not going to eat them," I said. "The gators will."

I was in heaven living the life of a performer. The first paid actor Houma ever had. I was also chasing the dream in a badass bachelor pad with a pool in my bedroom. I had the stage, the lights, and scotch. People were noticing.

I was doing stand-up comedy on a Tuesday when I let my guard down. In she walked, tall, young and slender. I thought she was exquisite. How could she miss if she wanted Big Larr?

When she entered the club, she glided across the floor like Morticia from the Adams family, not placing one foot in front of the other, but floating, and it seemed as if things just moved from her path. I was in the middle of my stand up routine, and I lost my place.

She had beautiful red hair and big blue eyes and back then if you introduced me to a red head, you could have first born. We were talking breeding purposes. I would gladly sell the little bastards.

I didn't pay her any mind after that, again I thought someone out of my league. (The last woman that was out of my league had me playing a gay guy, and this straight man wasn't playing that anymore.)

Days went by and I went about my business doing the show with her coming into the club. I admired her but only getting her name, Jessica. I was finally introduced to her and that's when she told me she wanted to be on stage. I thought, "Blow and behold," I'm sorry "Low and behold," I had a perfect place for her.

I would play Roy Orbison and she would be the "Pretty Woman." Just like the song. I'll sing dressed as Roy with the dark shades and wig, and she would just act out the lines.

Pretty woman, walking down the street,
Pretty woman, the kind I'd like to meet

It worked better then we rehearsed.

I was crazy about her. She was funny, charming, and wanted to be on stage. I liked her so much I was scared, but what scared me most was the fact that she was young. I liked older women when I was young. Holy crap! I was now old enough to have a relationship with a "younger woman."

We danced, we sang, we acted together. She even got in on the dances with the Illusions troupe, and she became best friends with the choreographer.

We fell in love.

It was great. She wanted to be with me all the time. She wanted to direct the show and I perceived that overture as she wanted to be a part of my life; my whole life and that thrilled me beyond my dreams. I was getting older but the dream of making it was still alive. Finally, I found someone I could take along for the ride. The ride to the top would be with Jessica, the first person I couldn't live without. I got her a ring, and we were going to be married. She then moved in my, "house with the pool."

That's when the fighting started. No longer could the dancers rehearse with me. She was also very suspicious of the new female performers when they auditioned for the show. She didn't want me working with other women in the show, especially the ones I worked with from the start. She even hated the "house with the pool." I quote, "You've slept with every woman who's been in here."

"No, dear. Not every woman. Some of them wouldn't let me."

When she told me she was going to cut me off sexually, I told her, "You can't. You're not smart enough to find the bitch I'm screwing." Geoff told me that one.

That's when I did it. The move I thought I would never make. I gave up the dream. I was willing to settle.
I was deeply in love for the first time, a feeling I'll never forget. I would have actually taken a bullet for Jessica. I would throw myself in front of it.

"Take me, not her." Life could not be without this one.

Until that time I had never felt the glow of total contentment, the undying love for just one person. But to be totally honest, she was getting extremely bored with me.

She was young, twenty-one, and ready for fun. I was thirty, and I took the local celebrity-ism seriously.

I was in the public's eye, getting noticed, and I acted like it. I wasn't getting crazy and acting silly because I treated the notoriety as I would if I was at a higher level. I figured if I couldn't act like it was real, at this stage, I couldn't maintain the level when I reached it. I took this performing thing seriously, and she didn't take me seriously.

"Who do you think you are?" was the way she put it. "Everybody thinks you're an ass-hole," That hurt.

I tried to clip her wings, and she resented it like everyone would. Our ages caught up with us just like they did with Veronica. This time I was on the receiving end so I decided to fight harder and do what a man in love would do. I gave more.

I spoke to the new owners of the radio station who had taken over the station two years earlier. The new program director said to come by, they'll hire me back to do the midday slot on C-107.5, the station I had left. It now had a country music format. I took that job and left the stage that I loved, but now I was at home, waiting for the one I loved. We ended the relationship four weeks before the wedding, which we both agreed on.

Here is the lesson learned. Don't give up the dream if someone doesn't believe in you, any dream, not just show business. Believe in your passion. I remembered Mother Mary wanting to be a famous fashion designer, but love and family got in the way.

At that time Jessica and I were two people who wanted something different. I wanted to perform and be known for what I do, and she didn't understand what goes along with being in love with someone who has the dream. Ask any family man or woman who wanted to be noticed. It takes a significant other who understands the passion. Yes, someone letting you be delusional. Jessica didn't want to be tied down to chasing my dream.

I will say this. She was right about feeling uncomfortable in the house. The house was a bit "see through." With the moon roof and the open glass, she constantly said, "It feels like someone's watching me."

"You're crazy; no one wants to see us."

"It just feels that way," she would say. I'd dismiss it not helping my cause to keep her.

One night about 3 A.M. we were in bed watching television, I grabbed the remote and turned off the TV. The house went completely dark, and the streetlight cast a shadow of a man's head on the window as it dipped it below the sill.

"Larry, did you see that," she whispered.

"Ya, damn right I saw that." I went to the front door.

When I got there, I thought to myself I'd better put some clothes on and went back for my robe.

I whispered to Jessica, "I'm going out the back and then around to the front. He won't notice me."

As I was making my way, I realized that I wouldn't be quick enough, and he might get away so I stopped and went back to the front door. This gave him time. When I opened the door, he was walking away down the street with his back to me. I turned around and said to Jessica, "I'm going to catch him."

"He might have a gun."

"Oh! Shit," I thought and walked slowly out of the house toward him. He was a light haired guy with a denim jacket; he was kind of small and had his hands in his coat pockets. I couldn't quite make him out because of the shadows, but I figured I could take him. I was about thirty yards away and thought if he pointed something at me I would just fall to the ground, but instead I yelled, "Hey!" He turned his head and our eyes met.

It was on.

He bolted down the street. I took off after him. My robe opened, and I was running as fast as I could, every secret below my waist was now shaking in the wind. It was cold and there was shrinkage, but I didn't care because I was in a foot race with a Peeping Tom down my street, and I was going to get that son-of-a-bitch.

He cut between two houses and in what seemed like one giant leap jumped a wooden fence. I could hear a big crash on the other side when he fell into some tin. Big dogs started barking with a fierce sound that made me feel that the dogs were going to get him.

I could hear yells of distress as he fought off the animals and then the sound stopped. The dogs continued to bark, furiously, but when I got to the fence, I decided I wasn't going in. The fucker was gone. I hoped with an ass full of a big dog's teeth.

When I walked back to my house, Jessica was in the driveway with her arms folded, and I was told, "I told you so," over, and over, and over again, and I promised I'd always believe her. We called the cops so it's on the record.

To this day, ask any of my friends. I don't like open windows at night and say "Bullshit" to people with a "no one is looking" attitude. That Peeping Tom screwed with my brain. Every window in my house is now completely covered. Maybe that could be a new show on HGTV- "Peeping Toms." That's an angle in home ownership they haven't explored.

I was back on the radio and Illusions, it lasted another few months. Lenny went back into the oilfield, and although I wasn't in New Orleans the Houma airways had me again. That plan to get back home was shot to hell. But, I was still doing plays and musicals, television commercials and even got my picture on a billboard saying Larry Hyatt was now on C-107.5.

I was chasing the dream once more and still trying to get the hell out of Houma, always leaving tomorrow. I'm thirty-two, and the doors are opening to a life on the road, a road that would teach more. Go figure.

Take It On The Road

The Illusions stage, the dressing room full of costumes, the light-up mirror, the dancing girls, the free scotch, my actor friends, and the extra cash were gone. I then told my family I was not getting married. That didn't surprise them.

My dream life was over, given away for love, and I was going back to chasing stardom in radio, playing the local celebrity, having learned a lesson, "I'm going to have to try harder." That's when a guy I knew from Illusions heard I was available and wanted me to compliment his idea. (It sounded very familiar.)

He wanted me to MC his karaoke night at different clubs in the city.

You see, now I've become a local veteran. The twenty-something crowd knew me from Illusions. My peers and the older generation knew who I was from the plays or as a country music disc jockey and the Swap Shop.

Maybe this performing thing might pay off after all. Illusions had the first karaoke machines in Houma, and this guy owned it. We had started karaoke after what we called, "The Comedy Zone/ Comedy Night with Larry Hyatt."

Damn good comedians performed on those Tuesday nights. One you'd remember was Carrot Top. He was an up and coming comic on the Comedy Zone circuit. I got to meet and hang out with these comics after the show, the ones that drank anyway, trying to take away anything I could learn from professional performers who had seen more than I.

Aaron became the third person in Houma I was blessed with. He was much like Geoff and Lenny because Aaron wasn't a "front guy." They were the businessmen and the back stage part of chasing a dream. I was an entertainer, a person who gets the patrons to enjoy themselves while spending money for the business people. I didn't mind that at all. Mother Mary taught us how to be creative. She didn't teach us how to make money. But, that was fine. My day will come, right?

Aaron's idea went like this: While the audience was watching karaoke singers, all of a sudden Elton John, Joe Cocker, Meatloaf, Frank Sinatra, or anyone of the artists I impersonated appeared on stage. It broke the endless, monotonous stream of karaoke singers. It sounded good to me. It sounded familiar.

When it was time to do a "skit" as people called it, Aaron would play dance music and get the place hopping and I would go get dressed as fast as I could.

We also invented karaoke characters as we went along. People we pretended to come out of the audience. One character was "Buck Nekked," a name Geoff thought would work. "Buck Nekked" was a very disgusting fellow with bad teeth and hair. He would sing Jimmy Buffet's, "Why Don't We Get Drunk and Screw," while trying to pick up girls in the audience. He used very disgusting gestures and very lude mannerisms. As time went on women who knew me would throw drinks on me and would get up and leave pissed off. People who didn't see the bit before would think, "What the hell is going on with this person." It worked. I didn't leave anything to chance. I was a showman, and I'll be damned if my audience wouldn't get a good show.

The show on the road was a hit. We went from town to town and club-to-club lugging the costumes and make-up. I was an added attraction. Aaron's karaoke machine came with a stage show.

Some bars were a little better than others. Some were complete dives, but always the dressing room seemed to be a closet. If I forgot to bring soap to take off the make-up, I used Ajax or whatever cleaner they had sitting on the shelf. I was still young and my skin at the time didn't know better, but I was performing, and gaining momentum. Henny Youngman's line, "I don't need a new act. I need a new audience," was true. I had my new audience.

When the skit was over, I got back in the street clothes as fast as I could, the dance music stopped, and I'd take the microphone and begin introducing singers, then back to the closet to start the process again. Just like Illusions.

A staple of the karaoke tour was the Ramada Inn. We played there two nights a week, Tuesdays and Saturdays. On Saturday I was lucky enough to use one of the rooms as a dressing room, right off the door where I entered into the lounge. Shit, I thought I was in Vegas. I would spread all my costumes out in the room and got the biggest kick out of getting calls on the phone from Aaron saying, "Larry… five minutes." Damn, that made me laugh. I got to stay overnight in the room after the show. Those times made us laugh until sun up.

Also, during this period, "The house with the pool in it," had gotten a bit small. That's how people we met in the street referred to Geoff's and my house. Through the years the fact that the house had no walls would sort of fix itself when Geoff would get married and move out, and I would take over the house. Or, I would go live with someone and Geoff would pay the rent.

This flip-flop of the house and Geoff repeatedly getting married had worked very well. You see, Geoff always seemed to want to have a wife and take his relationships to that level. I, on the other hand, wouldn't take the plunge, possibly because I was the product of divorce or had been looking for that feeling that once told me, "You are in love."

There were plenty of wives who enjoyed the hell out of Geoff and why wouldn't they?

His "completely out of nowhere" wife was the butch lesbian from Texas.

The one he loved most was the stripper he met in Houma who reinvented herself into a socialite after she hooked him and moved to Galveston; that hurt him.

The "OMG" wife was the girl with narcolepsy. He married her after she fell asleep at the Key Club on the sofa in the back and when security tried to move her, her leg came off. Can you imagine going to move someone who's passed out and off comes their leg? She was a narcoleptic with one leg that fell asleep in a bar. If she was Jewish and walked in with a rabbi, it would have been a perfect set-up to a joke.

He was also married to a "disc jockey" he worked with before I met him and would marry a communications student when he had just entered college. You already know about Veronica.

Geoff and I had never intended to keep the house as long as we did but for now he was a captain on a boat, living in Texas, disillusioned by years of people sucking up his talent for pennies. Doing very well, he worked twenty-eight days at a stretch and two weeks off, in the house was a situation that was good for two guys who thought the world of one another. I'm thirty-four, and Lenny comes back into the picture.

...

Lenny approached me about starting a new adventure for Houma, a playhouse, or a monthly arts and entertainment magazine that features theatre, music, dining and the arts. We would rent a building and produce plays that consonantly rotate a new stage show. With that idea I suggested we do children's theatre in the day, more adult shows at night, throw in a lounge, add poker machines, and Viola! My little bar act would be legit.

We decided that a playhouse would lose too much money at the beginning and went for the magazine. He ran nightclubs before, and together, with an editor, we should be able to pull off something worth reading. I asked him for a notebook with all the particulars but he concluded, "Larry, I'm way past writing your name down."

Geoff and I produced a mock copy of an entertainment magazine complete with funny stories, funny ads, and satire wit. The mock copy sold enough ads to get ads, and we were ready to begin. Imagine me, a remedial English idiot, writing a magazine. Damn! What a country?

We hired an up and coming writer, Sally, from the Houma Daily Courier which now comes out on Saturday. It actually was a daily paper and got after it, the first issue written in Lenny's garage.

As creative director, I decided the whole premise for the magazine would be informative and go for the joke. I understood that each year it would repeat the same information, something I had learned from writing the same radio copy each year. How many times can you say, "Festival, food, family, and fun," and not sound repetitious? You can't. Go for the joke.

I also told all the writers that funny headlines and humor was what we were after. Write two paragraphs and then start your story. I borrowed from Men's Heath when I told Geoff about an advice column called "Jimmie the Bartender." He gave good, down to earth advice with an "across the bar," kind of flare. He said, "I can do that, and I'll make 'em laugh."

"I have no doubt you will, Geoff. Please, don't get us busted." Then he would just fax us his column from the boat he was on from anywhere in the world. My buddy was still making me shine from far away.

With the first issue completed, we were on our way to New Orleans to meet the layout artists, and we still hadn't come up with a name. We're throwing out, "Houma Grown Arts and Entertainment, a take-off of home grown. "Tri-Parish Entertainment" and, "The Arts… By-You," which I thought was kind of cool being that we live on the bayou.

About 5 miles with time running out, Lenny said, "How about The Navigator?"

"It sounds like an airplane magazine."

"You don't like that? The Navigator?"

"It sucks, dude."

He seemed a bit deflated, "Really? The Navigator?"

"No! Not in your life!"

He leaned around his driver's side seat and grabbed a discarded envelope off the floor of his car, turned back, and asked Sally to give him the pen that was in the stack of ads, stories, and future jokes that would become my new outlet. He wrote down:

"The Navi-Gator'
Yes!
Lenny came through for me again.

...

Writing this arts and entertainment magazine gave me a very new perspective on what my life as a performer was becoming. I'm now entertaining the thought that maybe: I wasn't born to make a mark in the performing aspects of the arts. Maybe the teacher was right. I should be a businessman and possibly bring to life and promote the arts in this small town of fishing, crabbing, and oilfield families.

Was I realizing my fate was to have learned all that I have and come here to spread the arts in a place that didn't have the glee clubs, opera teachers, and enough gay guys to pull off a great musical? Maybe that's it? Could that be my calling?

Anyway, it was time to promote the magazine with not a dime to our name.

We came up with a genius idea, to walk the festivals handing out the first edition of the new "Tri-Parish Navi-Gator."

Lenny hired a beautiful model. She must have been six feet tall, dressed in a very sexy, short white dress, to walk along with me dressed in an alligator suit. It was August, and I, dressed like an alligator in the scorching sun, became a real problem.

I had forgotten the ice pack vest that goes under this monstrosity and went into the afternoon heat with nothing to combat the high temperature. The vest isn't an air-conditioner but with the ice strips that you put in the vest it keeps you from getting extremely overheated.

Everything was going well. The festival covered the entire downtown Houma area, and the picturesque streets were packed with people of all ages. One could barely make it from one block to another. All around, the festival's colors and sounds were trumpeting through the historic district.

The plan was working. The men were hanging around because of the beautiful model, the kids were hanging around trying to touch the costume, and take pictures with the alligator. All this as it got hotter by the moment. The sun beating down was something furious.

In time the evitable happen. I started to succumb to the heat, and with the weight of the costume, I started to get dizzy. It became too much for me to handle.

I said to the model, "I have to get this damned alligator head off of me, or I'm going to pass out. I can't take it much longer."

I quickly started toward the car which was blocks away, knowing time was short. Children and parents were all around, and I could hear the muffled sounds of the festival through the costume but being a professional, I would not for any reason take the head off the gator and expose myself as a human to the kids, who were now pulling me down and trying to grab the long tail. My God, I was overheated and couldn't stand it anymore.

Things got even more chaotic when I started to move faster, trying to get out of the children's view, my steps getting larger and farther apart and with only fifty yards to the car I couldn't stand it anymore. I b-lined as quick as I could for the refuge of my vehicle, and believe me, it wasn't pretty. I looked like Godzilla trampling Tokyo as kids were now screaming, yelling, and crying out loud.

Inside the costume I could hear a little girl shout, "Daddy, he's going too fast. Get him to stop." I heard a man's voice yell, "Stop the son of a bitch. He's making my kid cry." Everything was starting to get black as I tried to make it to the car.

"Daddy! Daddy! Stop him! I want to pet the gator." I heard the man's voice again. "Jesus Christ, he's knocking over all the kids."

I turned to see if any of them had fallen, but I couldn't see because of the sweat in my eyes.

"I'll stop him," the guy said, and I felt the tail of the costume being pulled so I couldn't go forward. I kept trying and trying, using my weight to push onward to the car. I thought he might try to swing me around by the tail, so I gave a backhand at the height of my shoulders thinking the kids weren't that tall and smacked the guy in the head with the big paws of the costume. He let go of the tail, and I barreled on through the last part of the crowd.

I made it to the car and ripped off the head of the costume and lay down on the pavement by the wheel, completely out of breath. Knowing I wouldn't have made it much farther I said, "Screw this. We have to think of a better way, at least until winter."

…

But what created the most stir was when Lenny, Sally, and I were brainstorming in our new "Navi-Gator" office in downtown Houma trying to generate free publicity.

Geoff was with us in the garage working on his advice column called, "Gator-Neauxs." It's pronounced, "Gator-knows." This is Cajun Country, and everybody does use the clichéd' French spelling for their names and signs.

Lenny, from buying advertising at the #1 rock station Rock 98.6 in New Orleans, suggested we should ask "Gator-Neauxs" a question about that radio station and possibly they'll mention us on the air. That would be it, genius, right? Not yet.

Wally and J.J., my radio heroes as a teenager, the people I wanted to become, were on that station. Since my high school days, they went on to New York and were back. I still admired them and now knew what egos, especially among radio personalities, would do. I came up with this question for "Gator-Neauxs."

Dear Gator,

On the way to work my husband and I listen to 'Wally and J.J. in the Morning" on 98.6 WNOR. He loves them, and I hate them. I say there's six of them he says there are two. What do you think?

Name
Larose, LA.

We liked it, but we still didn't think that was enough to cause a stir so we took a cheap shot: the rumor I've always had to endure.

We also hear they're gay.

We hand it to Geoff to write a response. He reads it, laughs out loud, and asks, "Would you like to rip them a new ass-hole?"

"Geoff, please don't get us busted."

"Wait a minute. For one, they're public figures, and I would never say anything that wasn't absolutely true"
I shook my head and said, "Aw, shit."

His answer came out in the next issue of the Tri-Parish Navi-Gator:

Dear Name,

I've listened to "The Wally and J.J. Show," and I like them very much. They're radio gods. There are two of them. That's why they call themselves, "Wally and J.J." As far as them being gay, I know J.J. is not.

Geoff, my boy, genius.

The issue got to their desk, and they talked about it on the air for three days. Wally was going to sue. (I think he was playing it up.) J.J. was amused because we only insinuated about his partner. We couldn't buy publicity like that. Two of the funniest sons-of –bitches on the radio that I can remember listening to on the way to NOCCA got punked. I'm sorry I used you, gentlemen. Well, not really.

You are getting the last laugh though. You are the ones living your dream.

Hollywood South Does Houma

The Navi-Gator was a blast. I was writing about all aspects of the arts; theatre, dance, galleries, music, festivals, reviewing movies, and telling people where to go to find all the great things that I love. I was an ambassador for the arts and not the performer I intended to be. I still did the musicals and commercials and going for the joke in the magazine had us laughing each day, but the dream still played on my soul and I was still in the small town of Houma.

It brings to mind what I told my friend who was a big fan of my work. She said, "You're so talented. You should go to New York or Los Angeles. You could make it, if you tried." It was always flattering when people would say that.

Jackie was once a teenager who called me while I was on the radio in the very early years that was in no way crazy or nuts. Those early listeners were now grown, married, and had children of their own, some feeling quite silly about calling so often when they were young and impressionable. Jackie just wanted to see me, as often as I wanted to see myself, "make it," and to at the very least, try.

My comeback to her remark was, "If I went to L.A. or New York, then who would entertain you?"

I thought that was a good comeback, a brush off of something that I put on the back burner. The clock was ticking, but I was rather comfortable. I was a big fish in a small pond, but I still wanted out. After all, I was still chasing a childhood dream; still preparing myself for the introduction to the wealthy elite that would get me noticed and make me a star. Jackie would actually give me the chance to be in the movies.

"Crazy in Alabama" is the movie starring Melanie Griffith, Meat Loaf, Robert Wagner, Rod Steiger, Lucas Black, even Fannie Flagg had a role in this thing. It was a major motion picture directed by Melanie Griffith's husband, Antonio Banderas. Houma and the surrounding parishes would be used as 1960's Alabama.

Jackie worked for the location people and got me an audition as an Alabama police officer. By now, I looked redneck enough.

As a glorified extra whenever they needed a couple of cops, they called me and another actor named Randy. When they needed more, they called me, Randy, and as many as they needed. I spent about a month on the set at different locations in the Tri-Parish area and it was a blast. I listened and watched intently, and I learned volumes about how to make a major motion picture.

The first time on the set was a night shoot and another moment that I've always longed for. I would be on a major motion picture movie set.

I checked in and was told, "They need you in wardrobe and make-up," and if that wasn't surreal enough, that's where I saw Meat Loaf, who played the Sheriff in the movie. I thought what it would be like, getting ready to sing together in "The Rocky Horror Picture Show." To think, I used to pad my body and impersonate Meat Loaf at Illusions and sing "Paradise by the Dashboard Lights." We had a revolving car, sound effects, the whole nine yards, and I'm next to him. I was digging this.

I then went to wardrobe, and they fitted me for a cop uniform, gave me my gun and holster, nightstick, and badge, and I walked across a field just outside of the city limits of Houma.

They were filming a 60's racial riot scene, and they told me to walk behind Meat Loaf as a television reporter interviewed him about the riot.

There was fake smoke everywhere, and revolving lights that made the entire area look as if there were an enormous amount of cop cars, yet no police cars were in sight. Melanie Griffith was watching the filming of the scene; smoking a cigarette behind me to my right, and Antonia Banderas was seated in a director's chair to my left, not more than two feet away, and I hear him yell "action." My breath quickened, and I was in the freaking movies.

I was in complete awe the entire night. I was in a motion picture. Major stars were all around and special effects with cast and crew were everywhere. The cast dressed in 1960's clothes and with 1960's automobiles off to the side the illusion was complete. I paused for a moment to take it in. I thought I was dreaming. I thought I was in Hollywood; I was doing what I always hoped for, what I dreamed of. When I looked over my shoulder and saw the words, "Houma Trucking Company" spelled out in big white lights, high on a building that was blocks away, I felt myself double take. "My God, I haven't gone anywhere. I'm here, in Houma, and this is just a dream. I've got to go. I've got to get out of this town."

After the martini shot, which I learned was the last take of the night, still amazed at where I had been and what had happen, I went to the Key Club and was asked, "What's up?"

"I was just in a dream, a really amazing dream."

The cast and crew of "Crazy in Alabama" stayed for about a month, and I had the time of my life. I was called to play the cop at numerous locations. I went to kick ass parties and picnics and played baseball with some of the stars of the film. These people were very cool.

The writer of the book that the movie was based dubbed me "Meatball" since dressed in the cop outfit I looked like Meatloaf. I was lucky enough to be invited to an Oscar party at an old plantation home with part of the crew. I was beside myself when I got to watch people in the movie industry watch their peers on television on the biggest night of the movies, a very different experience for a small town local celebrity.

It was a night I'll never forget. When their friends and enemies in the industry, famous Hollywood actors, would appear on the Oscar Awards they would either hate them or love them. Out loud they would curse them, praise them, blast them for what they were wearing, throw things at the television, when their peers either won or lost, and talked about who was sleeping with whom on the movie sets they work on. They were dropping famous names of directors, producers, and movie stars. It was the coolest party I ever went to. I couldn't imagine being anywhere else.

When they wrapped, (Yes, I used movie lingo) I went back to my life in radio, plays, television commercials, and musicals. I was performing and doing what I loved also chasing that dream I've wanted all my life, but now I realize I'm running out of time, and want to get there. I finally want to get to the dream.

I decide to call Geoff to tell him I'm going to rent the house, go to Galveston, and finally take him up on the offer, and maybe try this thing called stardom. I want to break out of the cocoon. I'm ready. I'm facing fears, and even though he was living with a lesbian, I would tell him that with his writing ability and my experience, in all aspects of the entertainment world, I now feel comfortable enough, and ready to pack it up, and get after it.

His wife answers the phone and says, "Larry, I'm so glad you called. He's not doing well. We have some bad news, Geoff has cancer."

My jaw drops.

"He's going back to a Houma to take some more tests. His mother doesn't know but his aunt and uncle does, and they told his brothers."

"What the hell happened?"

"He was feeling pain in his shoulder. He thought he had pulled a muscle and finally went to have it looked at."

"Jesus Christ, Geoff." I put my hand on my forehead to take a moment, "Please call me when he gets here."

"Of course, he will. He wants to talk to you." That scared me.

I slowly put the phone back in the holder and started to pace undecidedly back and forth from the pool to the front door. I didn't know what to think. I kept going back and forth, half in denial and half trying to grasp the situation.

Coming back toward the front of the house, I glanced over and saw the type-writer that was placed next to the red cone-shaped fireplace that always made the house seem like a ski lodge. Through the years, on purpose, we didn't advance to a computer. We felt it would have cashed in all the dues we've paid.

I started to imagine us writing the morning show, him in his big chair behind the type-writer, and I, to his right on the sofa with all the papers, notes, and napkins from the Key Club scattered all around us. I thought of the mornings we spent driving down the bayou in the Cadillac, the top down, laughing and him telling me, "Don't worry about it; I don't inhale."

I said out loud to the pool, "Fuckin' Clinton."

When Funny Men Die, Less Funny Men Cry

When I walked through the door, Geoff perked up from his hospital bed and asked, "What's up Guido?" a name he called me through the years.

"I'm hanging in there, my Bro. What's up with you?"

"Oh, I'm fine" he said, "and if I'm lying, I'm dying." I smiled slightly.

"Aw shit, Larry, laugh out loud. That's a good one."

"Oh, that's good, really good!" And we both laughed. I now knew he was coming to grips with what he'd be going through.

"Come on, Guido. Take your best shot. You got it in ya?"

When comedians give you the go ahead, you take your best shot out of respect. I took a moment, tightened my lips, and thought of how upset I was when I first heard about his illness and that I wanted to call him the very next day but didn't have his telephone number.

"Go ahead, big Larr. Try me."

"Well, Geoff, I did want to call you after I spoke to the wife and see how you were, but I couldn't find your number. Then I realized... your number was up."

"You fuck!" he yelled.

I got nervous.

"I have taught you well."

"Well... Geoff..."

I wanted to say more, but that was all I could get out. My lips tightened and we stared at each other. He nodded, and we both remained silent. He spoke first.

"The doctors say I got six months to a year."

"Ah, screw them. What do they know?"

"How to make money. They want me to pay upfront."

I laughed and said, "You don't have any money. You blow it on new wives."

"Yeah, but none of them respect me so I'm good."

After a pause I asked, "What would you like to do, dude?"

"Well, when I get the hell out of here, I'm going to stay with my aunt and uncle. They have a lot of room over there, and our house is where I don't what to be."

"It's still yours," I said. "What would you like to do with it?"

"Do you mind getting rid of it?"

"Of course not, this was our investment. You're my friend. I'll do whatever you want."

"I owe some people some money, and I'd like to pay them back. We can sell it to my aunt and uncle, and we can both make out okay. You'll get some money and you won't have to leave until everything is over. You can trust my aunt and uncle."

"That sounds like a plan. I could pay off my car and credit card and I could be dept free, sounds good." Then I realize what he meant by "until everything is over." That's when I knew this wasn't funny anymore, and I understood the situation. My best friend is dying.

In two weeks we sold the house to his family. I didn't want to live there and moved to an apartment debt free. It made life much easier for an overweight starving artist who was in radio chasing a dream, you see, I wasn't living from paycheck to paycheck for the first time in my life.

I visited Geoff quite often at first but as the weeks went by he started to decline and didn't want visitors, just wanting to be alone with his new girlfriend. The wife went back to Texas. Only Geoff could get rid of a wife and find a girlfriend while dying.

We did get to write together, once more before he died. I am so very thankful.

Mother Mary's sixtieth birthday was coming up and I was asked to write a toast and some things about her life. I was now the family writer, speaker, and comedian at functions and religious holidays, so I asked Geoff for his help since he was always so much better. It had been such a long time since we'd sat down together to make people laugh.

When I first met Geoff, I thought it was the age difference that made him so much funnier. I thought being ten years older and knowing more about life, he had more knowledge to pull from. I always felt that as I got older I would be able to match his humor, creativity, and strange take on life. I knew I was one step left of normal and I thought I would eventually get to the middle, but it wasn't that way. I didn't realize that he would grow too. He would continue to listen, read, and study human nature to better understand how the performing mind works. He was a comic genius who didn't get to the place he wanted, and I was blessed to have him enter my life. All young performers please listen intently to the older veterans you work with. They were there before you. They had and still have the dream.

The last wonderful memory of my friend was him behind that manual Underwood typewriter tapping out the capital letters, double line spaced, with that box of endless yellow paper, on the patio of his aunt's house, me, trying to act as if no years had been spent, and him, very pale in his favorite red flannel bathrobe making jokes to say about Mother Mary.

I wished, like the old days, he wrote the funniest things I ever heard but that day the medicine had taken its toll. He wasn't completely there, and he typed what was thrown in the air but oddly enough, I was the one who punched the lines.

It didn't matter. He had made me laugh a million times, and for so many years that just being next to him brought back the days when for us everything was possible, everything was just a joke away, everything was within my grasp.

About three weeks later his aunt called. Geoff was asking for me. They didn't think he was going to last much longer, possibly a couple days, and if I wanted to say goodbye, do it as soon as I can.

Walking into the house, I was nervous. Upon entering his room I had to smile and shake my head when one of his ex-girlfriends was next to his bed and waved me over.

Geoff was unconscious, had an oxygen mask on his face, and was turned to the left side of the bed. I went there to be closer. I was pleased when his friend smiled and said, "Thanks for coming. He spoke about you Larry all the time."

"My God, I had to come."

"Hey. What's up dude?" I said softly, and he ex-haled out loud.

His girlfriend said, "I have some things to do. You can sit here," and pointed to the chair next to the bed and left the room.

I sat down on the end of the chair, close to the bed, and could hear him breathing slowly out of the clear mask that covered his nose and mouth. The elastic band was around the back of his head, his eyes shut.

Looking down I was so very sad.

I didn't know if Geoff could hear me, but I wanted to speak to him and let him know what I thought of him and thank him for all his help. Mother Mary said to me many years ago when my grandfather was dying, "Go ahead talk to him. The hearing is the last to go."

I imagined Geoff jumping up and saying something funny. Something that would let me know his wit was still the biggest thing in the room, but all I could hear was the muffled in and out sound of his breath and all I did was cry. I couldn't say a word. My only hope was that he read my mind and that somehow he knew what his friendship meant to me; somehow he knew what he did for me.

That was the last time I saw my friend.

Two days later I got the call from his uncle. Geoff had died. I knew he was to be cremated and would have a memorial service in a few months and that was that.

Just like that.

I'll see his family in a few months and that was that.

Just like that.

...

At the memorial service, which took place in the room where he died, I planned to say something about my best buddy and how much we shared, the many years of friendship and camaraderie through good times and bad, but I still couldn't get myself to speak. I was still so sad of the loss and afraid that if I tried to say something the words wouldn't be there.

One by one his ex-wives and even girlfriends had something to say. Very nice things, all complementing his wit that was prevalent each time you spoke to Geoff. Imagine that, three of his five ex-wives and three former lovers went to his memorial service.

I'm told women like guys with a sense of humor. If that's true, that's how funny that fucker was.

After sitting and listening to his boyhood shenanigans from his mother, his adolescent antics from his aunt and some stories of how he and his brothers were influenced by his exceptionally weird way of looking at the world, I did finally muster the courage to say something, but it came out somewhat silly and tear-filled. It was something that he often did in the Key Club that would upset people but thrilled him each time it happened. It was a statement Geoff left everywhere he went.

Geoff had a pseudonym that he wrote under long before the one we gave him for The Navi-Gator.

All through the community little quips were written on the bathroom walls of different bars and lounges, quips that were smart or dry, sayings that don't normally appeal to the average man who goes into the bathroom to enjoy the sayings of former urinators.

The kind of things Geoff would write would be, "It's Christmas, let's kill a tree and drag it inside." Something they wouldn't quite understand. Something off the wall, no pun intended.

Or, he would just flat out insult a person and their families with something like, "The Teen Miss Dulac Pageant was held last week and Laverne won the talent competition. She skinned a muskrat in sixty seconds." Under the quip he would always sign, "Buck Nek-ked." The name he let us use for the stage.

All through South Louisiana, especially in the Key Club, he would write these things and men would come out of the bathroom wanting to praise or beat the hell out of "Buck"

"Who the fuck is Buck?" It became a battle cry.

Men would get back to the bar and want to kill him or think he's a person they'd like to see run for president. They wanted to know who this person is who had all these sayings at all the places they go. They wanted to know who he was so they could kick the shit out of him and be done with it or laugh with him and tell him he was a crazy human being. To some it was tormenting to others he was speaking their mind.

When someone would get drunk and come out of the bathroom infuriated after reading a message from "Buck," Geoff would very non chalantly ease his hand up to the side of his head and slowly pull the pencil down from his ear and place it in his top pocket. If they mentioned it to me, I would go along with the distain of Buck.

Believe me, patrons in the Key Club wouldn't have had any problem kicking the shit out of someone, or anyone who they felt deserved it. With some of the things Geoff wrote, he deserved it. But no one knew Buck was Geoff; who, just like me learned a long time ago it is hard to "cut" funny.

Amazingly, Geoff and I, standing at the bar five days a week would have pens behind our ears writing on paper and napkins. Yet for years people didn't put two and two together. How did they not realize the guy at the bar with the pen writing, is the perceived asshole writing on the bathroom wall?

It was just another way that Geoff made people laugh and was one step ahead of everyone else.

…

The last wife did take his ashes to Galveston; the place that became his favorite and took pictures of him in the urn at different places in the city and at all his hangouts that I'm certain he enlightened with his humor and sick sense of normal. She then took him to the Gulf of Mexico and dumped him over the seawall. He would have thought that was extremely funny.

Geoff also believed in reincarnation.

When I first moved into his house and after one of our writing sessions at the Key Club, he wanted me to read a paperback by a woman he thought would make me see the afterlife a bit different.

I've never told this to anyone, but, he told me, he thought he was once Mozart. I know. I know. I know. But God is my judge. When I would plink out Mozart on my piano from an old simple book of classical music I saved from NOCCA, that son-of –a bitch would cry like a baby. Tears would stream down his face. I always wrote it off as just melancholy brought on from the fifty cent inspiration at Happy Hour.

Interestingly though, toward his last days he mentioned he wanted to speak to his father who had died when he was a teen-ager. It made the minister at the memorial service feel he did believe in the hereafter and that possibly some sort of heaven would be there when he died. I sure look forward to seeing him again.

I'll always miss my friend, Geoffrey Dupre, whom I found out after he had died changed the original spelling of his name from Jeffery Dupre. He legally changed it to the proper British spelling when he became eighteen.

My boy genius wanted to be noticed.

Your clock is ticking, too

For two years after Geoff's death I continued to play the local theatre veteran. Interestingly enough, the town had grown around me.

I was still leaving Houma tomorrow and what was to become nine months has now turned into twenty-five years. I've invested a lot in Cajun Country and its people have opened their arms, hugged me tightly, many times, and in many ways.

Time does pass, oh so quickly.

I'd been in front of an audience for 40 years and I knew deep down, if I keep taking this performing thing seriously, I'll get the break I'm looking for. I just know it. I can fulfill this dream. I just have to keep trying.

My resume is now substantial and in some people's eyes done it all, but still, Mother Mary continues to remind me, lovingly, I can't get a loan without a co-signer. Then all of a sudden, in my mother's words, "For Christ's sake," a television show enters the picture.

Being the local veteran and with all the things I've done in the past 40 freaking years, I guess finally I'm getting good at it, and with someone offering me a television show, it's pretty much a shoe in on what I would say, "Where do I sign?" I've wanted to be in television since I was on Johnny's Follies.

LCN-TV, a new cable television network with the corporate office in New Orleans, is going on the air and its casting department is looking for talent in Houma.

The Louisiana Connection Network will be a statewide network on cable systems that will create programs that promotes all things Louisiana. With the diversity of Louisiana, you could pull this off.

I made it through the audition and was then approached by the owner. I found out it's a guy I met years ago who worked in radio with Sal. I knew he had gone into television at a station in Houma and had worked there many years. Jaime, the owner of LCN, Sal, Ryan, and I, started our radio careers together many years ago. We all knew what it was like to struggle. Jaime and I hit it off immediately.

Jaime was back from Hollywood and had worked at major television networks. He came back to raise a family in Cajun Country. Many have come back to raise a family and bring their new found knowledge back to inspire and enhance what was left behind.

The new television program would take place inside a radio studio, much like the radio talent from around the country in major markets. Shows such as Don Imus, Howard Stern, or Rush Limbaugh's web show, but our niche' will be that our show is all-fake. It would be as if

"Frazier' never leaves the control room, a talk show sitcom that refers to all things Louisiana.

The hosts would be poignant or outrageous. The engineer would be a crazy character. The co-host could be a hot chick who while on the air would put her feet on the console and paint her toenails. The producer would buzz us and let us know the governor was on the line but we would let them wait while we blasted them about their policies.

Nothing was sacred. All the callers of course would be interesting or outlandish and everything we say would be about Louisiana or its residents or issues that affect the Louisiana viewer. A set was built. I put together a cast. We did the pilot and to my amazement it caught on.

We added characters that we invented along the way. My favorite was "Rudy", aka, Buck Nekked, the engineer. We had a running gag where he always had tools in his tool belt that were broke and had to go to his truck to get another one. He was remarkably like Geoff and with each joke that worked I missed him more.

I was at it again and learned lightning can strike many times if you just stay in the storm. The radio, Illusions, The Navigator, the theater, the plays I've written, and now the television all seem to be coming together. This is it. This is my shot.

The show, "W-S-H-T," would have a chance to expand. I was told by TV executives to "change the humor to national issues and broaden the base. We'll get a staff of writers and produce the show in Metairie where the sound stages are being built." Hearing that for the first time was unbelievable. We would use the soundstage where I was an extra in an episode of "The Big Easy" on The USA Network.

By now you can imagine my excitement. My dream was becoming reality. The money I've never made is now in my grasp. People who helped me through the years can be taken along for the ride and also compensated for the unconditional love, and the push I needed when I just didn't think I could go further. I'm going to sing "Messiah," I'm going to nail it. I'm not giving up. It's late in life. Time waits for no one, and I've waited entirely too long.

This time, I got the call. I'm going to New Orleans for a meeting.

...

The signing with corporate would be on a Monday, December 21st. I needed some moral support so I asked Lenny if he wanted to take the ride. Lenny, the other believer, beside Mother Mary, always wanted to see me do well. I knew with him by my side I would be at my best to take on the suits.

We decided to leave on the Friday before and make it a weekend. Both being huge Saints fans and with the Saints playing the Cowboy's that Saturday night, going 14 and 0, and on to the Super bowl, the two of us in New Orleans would have a great time.

I was nervous, still well aware that until the ink was dry it wasn't a done deal and I've learned in this business, it isn't a done deal until you're actually doing it. And then, it's still just a dream.

We packed up and left Houma at noon, ready to enjoy a great win and hang out in The Crescent City, go to the meeting on Monday, and head back to Houma.

The ride to New Orleans was filled with excitement, emotions, and male bonding. We reminisced about the Illusions acts. I reminded him of the notebook, we mentioned Geoff and how living without walls can be a metaphor about roommates and friends who help each other by bringing things to the table the other lacks.

I said to Lenny, "We should stay at the Hyatt. I'd love to walk in and tell them I'm Hyatt, staying at the Hyatt."

"If you married Paris Hilton, she'd be Paris Hilton-Hyatt."

I made the sound of a rim shot and said, "You do know I wasn't a Hyatt when I was born."

"Get the hell out of here."

"No really, I took the name Hyatt when I went into radio.

"Your ass."

With a smile I said, "I'm telling you Lenny, my mother named me Hyatt because that's where I was conceived... You might know my brother, Jimmy Motel 6... Yeah! my sister Kellie, 8 days in."

"You're an idiot."

We were enjoying the road trip and stopped off at Spar's, a restaurant and bar known for their Bloody Marys and at a Walmart. I always liked people watching in an out of town Walmart. That's where we bought overpriced Saints shirts and caps.

I never wore caps because of the vanity of having red hair. I never liked to cover it because my hair made me different. I learned to never look for people in a crowd. It was much easier for them to find me with the bright red glare on the top of my red hair. I did play golf so I thought I'd give the Saints hat away as a Christmas present to a golf buddy the following weekend.

Lenny and I got to the Hyatt, checked in, had dinner, and watched bowl games in the lounge on the coolest freaking TV that I've ever seen.

That evening, I stayed up to sip twelve year old scotch and stare at the new medium that I would shortly take me full circle from that day saying the pledge of allegiance. I was finally going into the true boyhood dream and it was the first time I gloated in years.

When I awoke for the Saints game, I was excited. I had trouble sleeping the night before because I kept going through scenarios of the meeting on Monday. What will I say when these men ask me this? What should I say when these men tell me that? I'd gone through these meetings but never before had the stakes been higher. I was scared to death but ready to face down my fears.

When Lenny and I met for breakfast, the weather was cold but the sunshine made it pleasant. All I wanted to do that day was enjoy the events surrounding the football game. I couldn't take care of the show or fix it, so I wasn't going to dwell on it. Today I would have the beauty of gloating all day.

I wore my new Drew Brees shirt and brought the hat but stuffed it in my back pocket because I always looked silly in a baseball cap. For some reason I wore them low to my face, the brim down toward my eyes. Actually, hats always made me look stupid.

It was about noon and with the kickoff that night Lenny and I decided to walk to the Dome and hang out on Poydras St. with the tailgaters and see what develops.

We were close to the Dome and noticed a huge commotion. It was Saints players arriving at the stadium. People were all around and the excitement was intense. Black and gold was everywhere. Local and national news and sports media was setting up so we muscled our way closer and as the players were greeting the crowd, fans were yelling to get autographs from the players.

As the players were going down the barricades I jumped in line and shoved my hat in front of the quarterback Drew Brees. He grabbed it, signed his name on the crown, handed it back to me, and went to the next guy along the barricade. I got back to Lenny who saw the whole thing, and he just smiled and said, "You got his autograph? You bastard. You won't even wear the hat."

"It's an omen, dude. I heard on the radio his autograph is worth two hundred and fifty bucks. It's on a Saints hat. If they win the Superbowl, I'm in the money," and popped it on my head. We did a high five and went down Poydras street.

The Saints couldn't lose now.

For the rest of the afternoon we hung at the Dome with the tailgaters and met all the crazy Saints fans. The news media was interviewing people and the entire area was highly charged.

We met Whistle Monster, who is basically a guy with a huge whistle on his head. We laughed about how many women wanted to blow him, and the black and gold pope, who I personally had bless my newly signed Saints hat.

We spoke to very well endowed nuns drinking daiquiri's and invited them to join us at the casino.

"No, we have to say a novena," one said.

"Yeah, at what strip club?" Lenny whispered to me.

"That's two habits I'd like to break," I said back.

"Shit, they would break you in two and have you praying to do it again."

"Penance, my friend. I can do penance." It was that kind of day.

It was getting late, but we still couldn't get inside the Dome. The French Quarter was a bit far, but the idea of going to Harrah's Casino was somewhat doable. I was enjoying my day. "What a day, what a day." It was before the big signing, in my boyhood home, "The city that care forgot."

As the sun was getting lower, we decided to meander toward the river. I knew the layout of downtown much better than Lenny so I suggested we get to River Walk then go toward Canal Street. We'd kill an hour and get back to watch the Saints go 14-0.

On the riverside of Tchopitoulous and getting closer to Harrah's, we realized the shortest distant to the corner was to cross in the middle of the street and start toward the casino; the doors that people rarely walked through.

As we approached, a group of young men seemed to come out of nowhere. The shorter one in front said, "That's a good looking Saints hat," then pulled a small gun out of his jacket, pointed it toward my chest, and pulled the trigger. I heard a pop.

As it kicked me back, I saw him point the gun at Lenny, and it miss fired. Lenny jumped toward him and tried to wrestle the gun away, but the others attacked.

When I fell to the ground, the Saints cap came off and one of the young men went straight for it, grabbed it, and yelled, "I got it!"

As they all started to run the fellow with the gun got about ten feet away, turned around and again pointed the barrel at Lenny who was going to chase them. He dropped to the ground. The gun miss fired once more. Lenny took three or four more steps toward them and stopped. He saw it was futile and turned to me.

Lenny's expression confused me. I could feel heat in my chest. I was shot. Everything was flashing. I kept blinking. I was very scared.

The last thing I remembered was looking up at Lenny. I heard him say each word very definite, "Oh- My -God!"

Black.

The Awakening

T'was the day after Christmas, early to most, about 4:45 in the morning. I'm up at that time because I'm a morning person, an optimist. "It's a new day and what will the world bring me?" is how I feel when the sun comes up. It also comes from years of getting up early to host a radio morning show. Plus, I'm a firm believer; "If you get up and get after it" you beat half the human population. It's a way of getting an edge without screwing over your fellow man.

I'm an entertainer, and I've only been fired from one job in my whole life. I'm proud of that. I get after it. That is my work ethic and people have come to know it. This holiday season I was up early in Walmart.

I walked in and the place was buzzing. I noticed everyone in all departments had on the blue shirts, blue and white name tags, and were busy stocking the shelves, and taking down Christmas displays. A large lady was cursing,

"Where the hell is Amber?"

I nodded to them, the typical Wal-Mart employees, all shapes and sizes, colors, hair lengths, and facial hair. The guy with a hair net over his beard behind the deli counter scared me.

I was there to pick up some things, one being toilet tissue, and wondered if anyone I know will see me. Buying certain items embarrasses me. It comes from being noticed in a grocery store. Stand there talking to a radio listener with toilet tissue and a can of Blue Runner Red Beans, you'll know what I mean.

I picked up Dawn dish detergent, went toward the donuts, which were completely out, and grabbed Dewey Gooey Cake. I'm figuring it's the holidays; I'll work it off later at the gym.

I started a diet before the first of the year. After years of failure I've resorted to the notion that it's not how you begin a new year. It's how you end the old one.

I notice my reflection in the mirrored donut case and realized I've lost a lot of weight. Actually, it was the best I've seen myself in years, and my hair seemed redder. I looked younger which I passed off as, "Damn, the light in Walmart is excellent."

With an armful of items and no cart, because a "buggy," as the elderly gentleman with white hair and white beard called, it was not in view, (the guy actually looked like St. Peter.) I proceeded to the checkout.

I sure as hell passed the self-check out because I have never gone through one without ticking off the people behind me, and I noticed that none of the numbers at the check-out were lit. So, I yelled to a couple of female employees on the other side, in that front alley were people would begin to wonder on which side of the building they parked.

"Are you guys even open?" I asked.

"No! We're not open, baby!" came the reply.

"When do you open?"

"Six"

My first thought was, "Crap its only 5 o'clock"

My second thought was, "Why didn't somebody tell me they're not." I was walking back and forth, up and down the aisle for Christ's sake. I must have passed twenty-five employees. All of them looked at me but none of them said a word. What the hell did they think? I worked here? I got on a pair jeans and a Saints shirt with a number 9 on my chest.

Shaking my head and contemplating what to do next I remembered the wife of a colleague who is a Walmart employee. She told me, at a somewhat recent Christmas party, that one of the worst parts of her job is putting the merchandise back on its correct rack. So, I decided not to just leave it in the only aisle with the cigarettes and put it back, myself.

As I was placing the items back, I was now trying to figure out why all these people when they saw me shopping didn't say, "Excuse me sir, you idiot, don't you see there are no customers in here. It was Christmas yesterday, and we're not open yet. Yes, you sir, with your toilet paper. Had a big meal did you? Needed paper? Did you have an extreme load of turkey and fixin's?

I shot back in my mind, "No! But when you got to go, you got to go and I'm glad I didn't need suppositories."

Walmart employees have always interested me since I applied at Walmart and didn't get hired. I applied while I was working for a radio station I thought would go under because of bad times. When I didn't get hired by the biggest retailer in the world, I wrote it off as, "At least I wasn't fired by the biggest retailer in the world," because I'm a guy who gets up early and gets after it.

I went into oilfield business for a short time when I got fed up with the radio industry sucking up my talent and was amazed at how men would talk on their cell phones and discuss the stuff they were supposed to be working on. As if that would do the trick.

At this particular oilfield company, this young guy said to me, "Larry, you always have your gloves on."

"I don't want to lose my job," I said. "When the boss comes out of that office, I either just put something down or I'm about to pick something up. Dude, don't you think it's harder to look like you're working then not do what the hell is in front of you? At least I look like I'm getting after it."

He said with a huge understanding, "Oh! Wow! I guess you're right"

I bet he ends up a CEO.

As I walked out of that Walmart, I happened to wave to a police officer, jumped into my car, started her up, left the parking lot, and passed a few other stores that were closed. I didn't feel offended because they had their lights out letting me know I wasn't allowed.

When I passed a convenient store called the Cloud Nine, I noticed it was open, so I got the Dawn, Heavenly Hash, and the Scott one-thousand sheet roll that always seems to last longer. Walking away I was good to go and ready for a delicious breakfast of leftover turkey and fixin's.

When I got to the house Geoff was sitting at the typewriter, I could smell the aroma of my favorite, cornbread dressing. I smelled it the second I opened the door.

Geoff was dressed in a white terrycloth robe which I thought odd. He always wore the red one. He was sitting in his big chair, leaning forward; typing, but yellow paper wasn't in the typewriter. The paper was also white.

"What did you do, bleach your robe?" I asked.

"No. This color suits me."

"What happened to the red one?"

"Purification," he said. I dismissed it as typical Geoff speak.

I started to put the groceries on the counter and threw him the Scott tissue.

"I didn't expect you so soon, Larr."

"I would have gotten here sooner if Wal-Mart wouldn't have jerked me around."

"It's that shirt. It's a Saints shirt. You confused them. How've you been?" he asked.

"Fine, kinda hungry. How are you?"

"Here, read this," and he pulled white paper out of the typewriter.

I smiled. When Geoff handed me the jokes for the day, I knew it was time to chase the dream, and he knew it always made me feel like I was in the game.

Printed on the paper was:

Do you remember where you were yesterday?

"I don't get it," I said. "Where's the punch line?"

"Guido, it was Christmas yesterday. Did you see your family?"

"Of course, I always do."

"But, do you remember?" He wanted me to think harder.

"Come to think of it, I don't. But, I do remember driving to New Orleans."

"Do you remember seeing me?"I chuckled.

"Geoff, in twelve years you've gone to see my family three times. They thought for the first six years we were in the closet."

He smiled and then got serious, "Do you remember, Lenny?"

"Yeah, I do. I remember him saying, "Oh- My-God," and my words stopped me short.

A sudden burst of pressure pushed my head back without lifting my feet and scenes in my life travel through me. I remembered performances as a child, musicals, radio, Illusions, television. I was swept away and somehow once again in my home with the pool, but things were now very strange.

I took a pause and asked Geoff quietly, "What's going on? We're not supposed to be here. Are we in the house again?"

"Look, we don't have much time. Let's see if this time, I can now show you the writing on the wall."

"What do you mean?"

"Larry, I've been watching, watching your life and many others, and I've discovered that unfortunately in yours, you didn't want to make waves. You also needed to be liked, by everyone, and to get there you were going to throw yourself into doing what you do best. "

Confused, I asked very slowly, and eloquently, without mincing words, "What the hell are you talking about?"

"I'm talking about you."

"Me?"

"Yes, you."

Backing up slowly I sat down on the sofa. I took a moment and looked around. I started to realize what had happened.

"Look, Geoff. Don't start telling me that wanting to be liked was a stupid thing to do. People admire others who are popular. I thought if I could do those things, I would be liked, too."

"Tell me, Guido. Did you ever remember not being scared of confrontation?"

"Yeah, when I was younger. I remember a cocky little kid who thought he had talent but only because everyone said he did."

"You thought it was cool?"

"I liked it. Until my sister told me I was getting too cocky. She said my friends were starting to dislike me "

"And what happened?"

"It scared the hell out of me so I changed. Damn, I was humbled just to have a talent after that."

"And you did people's bidding."

"I swore I'd be gracious to the people who would let me sing. I didn't want to lose the one thing I could do."

"Guido, did you learn anything from being all that gracious?"

"To appreciate the fact that not everyone gets a chance to do what I do and if people were willing to let me, I could make money, and be noticed."

"Oh, you were noticed, but did it get you your dream?"

"No. The dream was bigger than this, bigger than all this."

"Yeah," Geoff mocked. "Then keep on doing what you're doing Larry, They'll notice you forever."

"Look Geoff, don't screw with me dude. Okay, I doubt my ability. Geoff, my nemesis rears its ugly head each time I have to make the next step. At every show the fear in me was another hill I had to climb. It's the eye of the beast that I've looked into my entire life, the fear of failure, the fear of being alone, the fear of being perceived as stupid, the fear of not being liked for doing the only thing I can do well. I lived with the fear of failure and what did I do? I keep throwing myself into the public's eye. Was it wrong?"

"I liked it when I could help."

"I ask again, was it wrong?"

"I don't know, Guido. You tell me, you're the chicken shit."

"No! It wasn't wrong!" I fired back, walking toward him. "I kept exposing myself to failure to be who I am! Wanting to be what I am was stronger than the fear of failure!"

"You weren't a failure at getting women."

"Because I was in the public's eye!"

"You weren't a failure at getting invited to all the parties."

"Again, because, I was in the public's eye!"

"You weren't even a failure at making a living." I was now in his face. The first time I'd ever done that to Geoff.

"That's right! You stupid fucking prick?"

He yelled back, "Larry, you are scared of failure in the public's eye!"

"Fuck you, Geoff!

"What! A confrontation? Look at you, all fighting mad." He was mocking me, and I walked in the opposite direction not wanting to fight.

After a moment, Geoff smiled.

"Larry, how the hell can you reach for your dream being scared of what you don't know will or will not happen? Your life sure was one crazy dilemma."

I took a moment and absorbed what he said and confessed, "Okay, I'm an idiot, a glutton for punishment. I chased a dream that constantly scared the hell out of me. Is that why I didn't make it? Is that why I stayed in a small town? Was being mediocre enough? Geoff, people sucked up our talent. The dream lost you years ago, but I did get a life out of it. My life was all those good things, too. Wasn't it?... Please answer me Geoff... Wasn't it?"

"Yeah." He said with a grin. "Now, you truly know, Guido. Go ahead, get after it."

Again, I felt a force on my face pushing my head backward. I was falling down a long tunnel, traveling fast away from a light; only this time when I landed I felt enormous pain.

Lenny's face, looking down at me shown turmoil. He had grabbed my shoulders and propped them up with his arms. He was shouting my name and shaking me.

"Larry, wake up! You red haired, "Chucky Doll" looking son-of-a-bitch, you better not die!"

I looked through half open eyes and said, "Lenny, I think he shot me."

"Oh! He shot you. A bullet went through your shoulder."

"Did he get the hat?"

"Yeah! He got the freakin' hat."

"Damn, I wanted that hat. Why do they always take the hat?"

"It looked stupid anyway. You always wear it too low." I chuckled.

"Is an ambulance on the way?"

"Yeah!"

"Good, I don't want to miss the meeting," and I noticed the people all around in black and gold looking down at me, noticing I was shot.

...

It's quite remarkable how things work out, or don't and how things can take its course or go full circle with the family we're born into, and with people we're lucky enough or happen to meet.

A path is made by decisions we make or things in our lives we are fortunate or unfortunate enough to experience.

I was fortunate enough to live the dream from the moment I had it, from when I kept singing that first song as a child, not knowing what that wonderful feeling of contentment was and before knowing what I was going to, and especially not going to become.

Being allowed to enjoy that passion grew stronger with each memorized song, each line I delivered, each joke I told, the large and small audiences, the failures, the successes, and the friendships of those that I confided in and those told the true story of why and what I wanted to do with my life.

I must confess. Deep down through the years I knew exactly what I thought I was doing. I was alive and living my dream in my mind.

Where else could a star but in his own mind get away with the personal indiscretions I shoveled under the rug, not appearing in the tabloids, and enduring the paparazzi, not showing up in The National Enquirer and be labeled the alcoholic or the druggy, my stupid mistakes, and growing pains exposed for the world to see, my relationship problems, family problems, and all the crap that one doesn't want people to be aware of, only known if you read the police beat of the local paper.

I didn't make much money. But what is money? Well, it sure would have helped me get the few things I longed for, the trips I saw my friends take to Cancun, the Bahamas, or Europe. All around, people were going to their expensive camps in Dulac or summer homes in Grand Isle and I wished I had those things but I guess I didn't reach high or far enough. "Who would entertain you?" I rationalized.

But, I did have a cool ass bachelor pad, lifelong friends, and all the notoriety that came along with being a "somewhat" celebrity.

No, my life was relative to what was in my heart, nerve, and desire.

Is it a good thing? I may never know or even want to.

I think of other "wannabee's" who didn't have what I had or the "younger, up and coming," who envy my mediocre existence that I pretended was the celebrity world that I chase. To you, in the long run, I hope I entertained. I'll go so far as to say I hope I inspired you to become what I didn't or couldn't or wasn't ready for.

Continue and do it for you. Don't give up. That dream is not going to die.

The dream, or living it, also chased away the courage to leave Houma, a well-built cocoon that took years to weave, although questionably tight since I was always leaving tomorrow, my mediocrity being success.

Of course, living on desire and making only enough money to make ends meet chased away some wonderful people who I wanted to take for the ride. I remember one woman who years later told me she wouldn't go out with me because of my car, and it wasn't the one with the side-swipe. Go figure.

I never really blamed those who thought not having money was my short-coming. To put up with a man, his dream, and then add being broke to the mix is out of most women's comfort zone, especially now, at my age. It was heartwarming to learn that a woman, who I wasn't good enough for, ended up marrying the owner of one of the biggest grocery chains in the south. I wonder if she ever thinks of me... just kidding.

No, the only luxury I've never been afforded was the luxury of having luxury.

I will never give up. You won't either, if you know who you are, not in your mind anyway.

I lived a passion from the day I was born and through it all, good times and bad, paying the bills and not, good cars and side-swipes, a bedroom with a pool, sleeping in the car, people sucking up my talent and letting others prosper for it, being scared of confrontation, or falling for women who didn't accept me- my life went exactly how the little red haired kid with the midget milkman clothes was supposed to. Noticed me? They did.

THE END

UPDATE

Now, I've added writer to my resume, with this being my words, phrases, and things I've embellished and flat out lied about. Fiction is what this is and what I wanted to tell you about myself, my life, and the stories that came freely.

Those who know me well know what I've left out, what I've embellished, and what should have been put into the narrative. I thought it would be better saved for a second look.

I do want to say that this was done as a teaching tool for people who have chased the dream, like me from such an early age. Or, it's possibly one last shot.

I'll keep trying. That is if my wife decides to allow it. You see, there is more to this story. I've found my other true love and now balance a love for of the arts with a woman who is not impressed by them. The other side of living with a dreamer, from what I can see, is plenty of looking up, shaking your head, and rolling your eyes.

Larry Hyatt

THANK YOU

There have been many, who, unwittingly, took apart in this project. Please don't blame them. I would like to thank my wife Jodie, Sue Peace, Stephanie Kenny Gomez, Julie Chauvin, Stacey Weed, Glenda Toups, Terry Harris, Frankie Hebert Dupre, Celeste Breaux, Kevin Carress, Linda McNeil, Bill Boudreaux, George Beaudry, Caroline Starr Rose, Judy Brickfiel, Kellie Gironda, and the members of the Writer's Anonymous Group in Houma, who will remain, well... you understand.

—Larry